NEVER
FORGET YOU

Trigger Warnings: Death, violence, abuse and explicit language.

Not suitable for younger readers.

Copyright © 2024 Faith Fawcett

All rights reserved. No part of this book may be reproduced or used in any manner without the prior written permission of the copyright owner, except for the use of brief quotations in a book review.

Paperback: 9798321568040

First paperback edition July 2024

Cover art by Emma Smith
Graphics by Emma Smith and Faith Fawcett

For Christine

because we will never forget you

why do you carry so much sorrow in your heart when the world is full of wonder and beauty?

because all I wonder is; why she was taken from me. Since she's been gone sorrow took her place in my heart. Now the world does not seem so beautiful

Prologue
1 year before

"Mum?" I scream, racing down the hospital corridor. The lights are flickering above me as I run past nurses, bounding into a trolley and stumbling forward. They shouldn't have even left the stupid thing out here; the building is full of patients who are struggling to walk normally, let alone through this mess. I push it angrily into the wall, hearing a scuffle of metallic equipment hit the floor a second later.

"Excuse me!" someone complains.

But I ignore them. There are more important things happening right now; I need to find her. Make sure she's okay.

A few doors further down, I finally find the numbered room I'd been sent to. This is it.

This is her room.

"Mum?" I say again, this time quieter. My voice echoes into the emptiness as I see her limp body decorating the clinical bed sheets. She's been connected to a million tubes and her eyes are closed tightly, her face bruised to the point I barely recognise her... is she even conscious?

When the police rang, they didn't give me the details. All they had said was that there had been an accident and she'd been taken away in an ambulance...

"Don't hesitate to come down," he'd said. What does that even mean? During the phone call, I had thought it meant she wasn't going to make it; I needed to come quickly if I wanted to say my goodbyes. But looking at her now, there's no way she can be dead. She *can't* be.

I quietly tiptoe further into the room, not even bothering to close the door behind me. With each step, I hesitate a little, unsure of what I'm supposed to do. They never teach you about these things in school... how to deal with the possibility of losing the people you care about... maybe having to watch your own Mum die in front of your eyes.

I can work out the area of a damn circle, though.

Tense, I stand beside the bed, floating my eyes across her body. It makes me feel sick, seeing her like this, especially because I know she'd hate it. She's always smiling, yapping on about being positive and finding the good in things. Yet, here she is now: silent and hanging on for her life.

"Are you Gracie?"

I whip my head around to the doorway, jumping a little bit at suddenly being disturbed.

"You're the daughter?" he asks.

I nod my head.

"Good, I'm Doctor Brown. I've been looking after your mother."

"Do you want a medal or something?" I say, perhaps a little too quickly. I need to calm down but I'm so angry that this has happened to her. Out of everyone I know, she's the furthest from deserving this... it should be me instead. I'd take her place in a heartbeat.

He clears his throat awkwardly.

"I don't know how much the police told you on the phone," he begins. It sounds like a question, though, so I answer it.

"Nothing helpful," I say. "Just that she'd had an accident. What does that even mean?"

"Your mother *was* involved in an accident," he repeats. "Quite a serious one. She was in a car accident... it was a hit and run."

The words sink into me as I try to process them.

A car accident. A serious one.

"Will she be okay?" I ask.

"We're not sure yet," he admits. "She's got the best care available and we will be monitoring her for any changes twenty four/seven. You are welcome to stay as long as you like; though, visiting hours do end at four."

"That's not as long as I like then, is it?" I Mumble. He chooses to ignore me, placing the clipboard he has been holding into a little pouch on the wall beside the door.

"If you need anything, a member of staff will be able to assist you," he says and then turns to leave.

I rush from her side and slam the door behind him, shutting the world out as much as I can. But, I should be quieter... I don't want to disturb her and make her worse.

"I'm sorry," I say. I pull the chair to the side of my Mum and take a seat, holding her hand in mine. She probably can't even feel my skin against hers but I'm doing this is for me; I need her strength to get through this.

I sit like this for a while, watching the monotony of her still face for what could be hours. A few people have come in to check her charts and feel her pulse, but no one ever stays. Does that mean they're not worried about her? I hope it's a good thing.

"Gracie?" comes a hoarse whisper. Her lips move ever so slightly.

"Shhh," I say, beginning to tear up and tightening my grip on her fingers. I have to be strong for *her* now; I have to prove that I'm mature enough to handle this and be okay. Fifteen is old enough to do this, to understand. "Save your strength."

Her eyes flicker open, the familiarity of those brown irises swirling in my mind as I try to create a memory. If anything happens, I need to remember her as precisely as I can.

"I - ca - n't," she tries to say, each letter seeming more difficult than the last to get out.

"Can't what?" I ask her. "Can't *what*?"

"I lo - ve y - you," she stutters.

"I love you too, Mum," I say, proud of her for trying to push through this but she closes her eyes slowly. "No, you can't leave me! *Please* don't leave me! I can't do this without you…"

She's doesn't reply.

And then I hear it: that long, steady beep from the machine.

The one that means my Mum is dead.

PART ONE

Dear diary,

It's the anniversary of mum's death today.

Everyone keeps pestering me, trying to make sure that I'm okay. Apparently, I'm dealing with it really well but they've got no clue. Do they really think that this is something you can just get over? Like she didn't mean anything? Like she wasn't my best friend? They're stupid to even think it and they're worse for believing my lies.

Soon after the accident, it started to appear in the media. It's only a small town, so news travels fast, but I didn't expect it to take off like it did. No matter where I went, there was always some reminder of what had happened to her...

The pile of memorabilia plastered against the pavement where she had been hit...

The 'wanted' posters for the car they suspect had caused it but had never found...

The pitiful looks on people's faces once they realise who I am...

It may have been a year ago but I'm still living every day like it happened yesterday. I just want to get off this stupid merry-go-round and move on with my life. Find
a way to be happy again.

gracie

One

A lot has happened since my Mum died but none of it feels quite real. Since my Dad had buggered off and practically abandoned us both when I was little, she had left me all alone... I couldn't stay at home by myself so I was sent away reluctantly to my grandma's and the house was put up for sale.

Fast forward a year and I'm living with my Auntie Debbie (my gran was diagnosed with cancer and I became too much of a burden) and the house has been bought by a family with two children and a dog... the perfect little image, right? I still catch a bus over to Green Haven sometimes, peering as subtly as I can between the curtains, trying to make out her face in the glass.

I never can.

The only way I can picture her is seeing her lying in the hospital bed in those final moments, less than half of the person she used to be. She probably hates the fact that so many people saw her like that, all lifeless and numb. Everyone knows her as the bubbly florist. People will know Eve Myers as the small child who used to run around the surrounding fields, organising the flowers she had picked in her baskets.

That's my favourite thing about my Mum: she always knew what she wanted, who she wanted to be. And she never let anything stop her, or no one.

I wish I could be more like that... courageous. I talk a lot, people always say, but that's only to hide how I'm feeling. I've never really felt *seen* by anyone before, only her. Only my Mum.

And now she's gone.

I stare at the violet dress I'm wearing in my bedroom mirror, watching it pool around my black converse. She never minded that my style was a little all over the place, she actually liked it. Anything that meant I was finding myself was good by her. But Debbie will go nuts when she sees how I've put the outfit together, I'm calling it now.

"Oh, Gracie," she'll say with a disappointed head tilt. "Have you got anything else to wear?" she could ask, looking at my shoes like I'll trek mud all over the house. I only did that once, and that was because I'd forgotten to take them off because the rain outside had absolutely drenched me. She shouted about it for days afterwards, complaining that she'd never get the stain out of her brand new carpet.

I wish a carpet stain was my biggest problem.

Instead, I'm the girl with the dead Mum.

"You ready?" Debbie says, hovering in my doorway.

I turn to look at her slowly. I could stare at her in silence, refusing to speak; no one could blame me today.

"You told me to be ready for nine, so I am," I spit out harshly.

She clears her throat and I can tell that she wants to tell me off for being rude, but she can't. Not today. I've basically been given a free pass to do whatever I want because no one will speak out against me.

"Good," she says. "We're just heading there now."

"Give me a second," I tell her and she nods, leaving me to look at myself in the mirror again. I try to picture her stood behind me, combing her fingers through my hair to remove the tangles that my curls have already created.

My ringlets came from her. They must have, no matter what my Dad looks like, because she had such beautiful and bouncy ones. We were basically twins, except hers were always so much healthier than mine; at fourteen, I'd bleached it all so I could have purple hair, and it didn't go well. I had also stained half of the bathroom but she just laughed at me, saying next time she'd pay for me to go to the salon.

I never did go.

There wasn't time.

Because she was gone only a few months later.

Maybe I'll dye my hair purple one day in remembrance of her; a reminder that she always wanted me to be my own person, even if other people didn't like what that was.

But not now.

Today, I have to go to an event which is celebrating the life of Eve Myers, one year after she died in a tragic accident... and I have to put on a brave face for her.

I tuck my hair behind my ears and, with no surprise, a brown corkscrew falls back down across my cheek.

And I smile. Because she may not be here anymore, but I am.

"Gracie!" Debbie shouts up the stairs.

I guess I can't put it off any longer... I grab my canvas bag and throw it over my shoulder, trudging down the stairs with a smile on my face.

Even though I've lived here for a few months now, Auntie Debbie's house still doesn't feel like home to me. I suppose it never will because my heart will always be longing to be back with my Mum. This is just bricks and mortar... and some really terrible decoration.

At the bottom of the stairs, everyone is stood waiting for me. Auntie Debbie has clothed herself in a black pantsuit... Mum would have hated it because of how morbid it is. They were always so different, even when they were little. They may have looked related but their personalities couldn't have been further apart.

Then there's my Uncle Steve, sporting a suit; he has to leave early to head to work. He's rarely at home since he's the head of the office. There is always something going wrong, which is kind of concerning as it's an insurance company... I won't be applying with them when the time comes, that's for sure.

Brodie has his headphones on, shutting out the chaos that is his family. He's only a year older than me, but he acts like it's more; apparently I'm 'uncool' and I've 'ruined' his reputation among everyone at the academy. After the accident, I had to move schools as my previous one was too far away to travel to every morning... it was awful timing; I'd never felt more alone. But having Brodie around just made things worse; I thought it would die down once he started at the sixth form there but no one forgets things like this.

Tying his shoe laces on the bottom step is Dexter. Really, I should say 'tying and failing' because he's been learning for months and still can't quite manage it. His small five-year-old hands are too shaky to do it but I have to applaud his dedication.

I feel like an outsider stood beside them all now. Auntie Debbie may have been Eve's sister but they didn't even like each other; now she's been dumped with an extra daughter, an extra body to clothe and feed and raise.

"Let me help you, Dexter," Debbie says.

"No, no, no!" he screams back. He's never been one of the quiet ones but I actually like that about him because neither was I.

I've always been loud. Loud about who I am, what I want, what I *don't* want. It's been harder this year but I'm trying to hold on tightly to who I was before so that she doesn't fall under the cracks of the funeral casket. And it's bloody exhausting.

"Alright, alright," Debbie sighs. "Why don't you all get in the car and we'll be out in a minute."

No one bothers to reply with words. Instead, a small shuffle of feet ensues by the door as we all make our way outside and down the drive. It's November, so I can't be surprised at how bleak and foggy it is... I wish she had died in spring.

I mean, I wish she had never died at all, of course, but since she had to, I would rather it be at a beautiful time of the year. All the flowers would be out and shining, her garden would be alive... even if it's now being appreciated by a new family. I hope they didn't tear it out. I've never been able to check since it's weird, even by my standards, to go into someone's back garden without their permission. And I'm not exactly going to knock on their door and ask if I can see it because my dead Mum and I used to live here and I really miss her and all that jazz.

So, I pretend that it's still there, waiting for spring to call all the flowers again.

I stand awkwardly in the driveway, noticing some of the neighbours stood outside their front doors. They are looking directly at me, shaking their heads and holding their hands to their hearts as though they can understand a single morsel of what I'm feeling.

Well, fuck them.

Only I know what it's like to really and truly lose Eve Myers. She may have been loved by everyone in this stupid town but she was only ever a friend or an unwanted sister… I'm the only one who lost a Mum.

"You alright, love?" Steve claps his hand on my shoulders, realising that I haven't climbed into the car yet. "It's going to be a tough day but we can take it at your pace."

"I'm fine," I say, shrugging him off. "Let's just go."

I buckle myself into one of the backseats, next to Brodie in the middle. Dexter's car seat is filled up soon enough, the loud rumble of his complaints droning on.

As we take off, driving past all the curious eyes, I stare at my fingers on my lap, trying not to shake… trying not to cry. Mum always said she loved how strong I was but I don't feel like that anymore.

I've never felt weaker, actually.

Two

When we pull into the car park an hour later, I go numb. It's all feeling even more real now, reminding me of how less than a year ago, I'd been sat at her funeral. All I can hope is that not *everyone* is wearing black this time; she would have hated it so much. Eve Myers was the epitome of colour, bright and sunshine-y no matter how she felt. Apart from her last few hours on earth… whoever hit her, they stole the light from her when it mattered the most. I'll always hate them for it.

I click open the door and my shoes sink into the gravel, crunching beneath my feet.

"Move over," Brodie says, trying to squeeze past me.

I glare at him.

"Sorry," he mutters.

I hate the pity but I step away all the same. I don't want people being nice to me just because of what today is. It doesn't seem real or nice at all… I feel like a damn charity case.

Oh, poor Gracie, all alone without her Mum.

What a shame; she was such a lovely woman.

Hopefully she won't head down the wrong path now…

Hang on a second. That last one isn't my imagination. Two elderly women are stood a few feet away, twittering to each other as they look in my direction.

"It happens, you know," the one with the bird-nest-hair says. "She won't have a good role model now."

"I think I'll be alright," I shout at them, calling them out for their rudeness. Did they really think that I wouldn't be able to hear them from here? I may be mourning but I'm not deaf.

The two of them look a little uncomfortable and maybe I should care a little bit that I've just shouted at two little old ladies but they were in the wrong. You can't just talk about me like that and expect me to be cool with it.

"Let's head inside, see who's here," Debbie says, locking the car up and grabbing Dexter's hand before he can try to run away. He's literally the devil child. But Brodie isn't too far from that, either. They're both a bunch of weirdos that I unfortunately have to be stuck with.

I follow after them all, standing back a little. It's the same venue where the funeral was held; they do a discount if you book again for an anniversary event. It's morbid but Debbie and Steve insisted on it, saying that if they were going to do it, they best do it properly. And how can I argue with that? I can't exactly say that she doesn't deserve a second send-off; hell, even two isn't enough to do her justice.

Seeing all the flowers inside... blacks and navies... makes me want to vomit. It feels like an offense against one of her favourite things, another thing stolen from her because someone didn't care enough to swerve out of the damn way.

I want to rip them out of their stands and stamp on them in my converse, showing everyone how little they knew her. They haven't a clue about what she was really like, no matter how much they pretend that they were 'so close' and 'loved her so much'. Everyone here - *every single person* - doesn't care about her like I do. They've only shown up so that they can appear to be a good citizen.

I don't have the luxury of pretending.

Debbie and Steve start making the rounds, leaving Brodie and I to watch over Dexter.

"You good?" Brodie asks, nodding his head at me.

"What do you care?" I wince back at him, folding my arms and creasing my dress.

"It's weird, isn't it?" he asks. "Everyone's here because Eve is dead."

"You did not just say that," I say, staring at him in surprise. Yes, I've been thinking it but *I'm* allowed to. I'm the daughter of the damn deceased.

"Its' just how it is," he replies, shrugging his shoulders. "You want to get food? Dexter, you want food, right?"

Dexter nods enthusiastically but I just shake my head in disbelief.

"You two can," I say. "I'm going to the toilet." I don't really need to go; I just want to get out of this room for a minute.

He doesn't follow after me. My guess is because he doesn't want to... he might have to watch his annoying little brother, but I'm sixteen. I don't need a babysitter.

I remember where the toilets are from the last time that I was here. I spent so much time in them, puking into the bowl, holding my own hair back. And now I'm back... all alone *again*.

It's quiet in here and all the stalls are unlocked. Good. I choose the one in the furthest corner, locking it behind me and hanging my little white bag on the back of the door. Shuffling everything around to get to the bottom, I pull out the packet of cigarettes and lighter I'd buried.

I still remember the first one I'd taken. Brodie and his friends were all hanging out in the back garden, camping out in the shed. I'd come in to bring them the snacks that Debbie had prepared for them all but they'd asked me to stay.

"Just a few minutes," I agreed, though I wasn't in the most social of moods. The accident had only happened about three months before and it was my first week of living with my cousins.

The boys all had their own cigarettes and it seemed to be their main activity. One of them even offered one to me... I'd said no at first, saying I wasn't stupid enough to dabble with stuff like that.

But then it got me thinking… it was a way to forget for a moment. A method to find some peace.

So I had one. And from there, I always found a way of making sure I had a packet on me for when times got really hard. I don't have a lot… I'm not addicted or anything. But some days are harder than others and I don't want to hurt.

She'd be so disappointed in me but I don't believe in all that bull about how she's looking down on me. So, does it really matter?

I get so annoyed when other people disrespect her memory but who am I to talk? I've become such a let-down of a daughter… there's no way for me to make up for that now.

And so I light another, sitting myself on the tank of the toilet, resting my feet on the seat. I chose this cubicle because I remembered it had a window; I don't know how sensitive the smoke alarms here but I'm not risking anything. Though, I don't think I could get in too much trouble, not today of all days.

I take my first puff, relinquishing myself to the nicotine and blowing out the smoke softly. It already feels so calming but there's still a knot in my stomach, twisting slowly around my organs.

No, don't think about organs… hers failed her.

Because of a random person who took a life but didn't care enough to own up.

I don't know if I'll ever get answers… the inquiry is still open but I don't think there's much chance of finding anything after this long. Maybe they won't be able to face their guilt... they'll march themselves into the police station and admit to everything.

Unlikely.

I have to accept the fact that my mother's death will remain a mystery, even if it rips my heart out every time I think about it.

"Anyone in here?" I hear a door and then a voice. I put the cigarette out, twisting it against the window sill and chucking it onto the ground outside.

"Just me," I say, trying not to cough on the fumes now that I have an audience.

"Gracie?" It's Zoe... a girl from school. I haven't spoken to her much, mainly because I tend to avoid everyone. Either that, or I never quite make it to the school gates. "Are you okay?"

"I'm fine," I say back, holding my breath for some reason.

"Have you been smoking?" she asks.

"Uhm, no," I lie, wafting my hand around to clear the air more.

"It's okay," she says. "I don't blame you."

"You don't?" I whisper.

"Of course not," she answers. "Today must be awful for you; I can't even imagine how you're feeling."

I step down off the toilet and stare at the lock, my fingers hesitating by it. I don't let people in anymore... if you love people, it only hurts more when you lose them. But I don't have to get attached.

Besides, it might be nice to have someone around today, someone my age.

"You won't tell anyone, will you?" I ask, opening the door. I must look a right mess now... but she doesn't even glance down at my converse.

"Promise I won't." She looks stunning, sporting a floral dress, looking older than just sixteen. Mum would have loved it, how bright the colours are... the intricate pattern.

"Did you know my Mum was a florist?" I say.

"I don't really know anything about her," she admits. "I thought you could use a friend at this thing."

"You travelled an hour for me?" I ask. "Why would you do that?"

"On a bus too... No one should have to go through these things but, for whatever reason, you do," she says. "I can't turn back the time to bring your Mum back but I could do the right thing and try to make it easier for you."

"We're not even friends," I say, regaining some of my usual mood. She doesn't make any sense at all; why would she come all the way out here when she's got nothing to gain.

"Not yet," she smiles. "Come on, they've got pizza!"

"I do love pizza..." I bite my lip. "Okay, fine. But I don't want to talk to everyone and hear their fake ass condolences."

31

"No problem at all," she says. "If anyone tries, I'll just explain that you're too upset to talk right now."

"You know what, I like you, Zoe," I decide.

"Why, thank you, Gracie," she jokes. "Come on, let's get you a slice."

She holds out her hand, and, for the first time in a very long time, I let someone in.

Three

Heading back into the event makes me feel like I'm voluntarily sending myself as a tribute into some courageous battlefield. But it's lighter with Zoe there, even if she is practically a complete stranger.

We charge through the crowds of people, weaving between them and heading towards the back corner where the buffet has been set up. Barely anyone has touched it yet by the looks of it; they probably think it's disrespectful but I don't have to worry about that.

"What pizza do you want?" Zoe says as we look at the selection. "My favourite is always pepperoni. I guess I'm pretty basic."

"Nothing wrong with basic," I say, taking a slice. "It's my favourite too. Go on, grab one; don't make me do this by myself."

"I'm absolutely starving," she complains, taking a bite. "I never like to eat in the morning; it makes me feel ill."

"Same here," I say but it's probably for a different reason.

Sometimes I feel guilty… you know, eating when she can't and never will again. It seems wrong and it makes me wonder why I'm still here and she isn't. What makes it worse is that none of it even needed to happen. If she had stayed at the shop later than evening... or if the driver had never got in their car... Even if they had set off a minute later, would my Mum still be here? Still be alive?

I'll never know for certain but it feels pretty damn likely. Hit and run's aren't exactly common, especially here in Green Haven. It's so small that everyone knows practically everyone; you can't slip between the cracks here, even if you wanted to. It makes me think that the person who killed her must have just been driving through... someone would know something otherwise.

Their identity would have easily been discovered.

I'd know who murdered my Mum.

Even if it had been an accident, why not just step forward? How can you live with yourself knowing what you've done? She was all over the news, the TV too... they will have seen her, seen the street where it happened, where everyone left balloons... They *will* know.

But they're a coward.

"So, what happens at these things?" Zoe asks through a mouthful of pizza.

"I don't know," I admit. "It's my first one. I didn't really want to come but I think I have to be here."

"I get you," she answers. "You'd probably feel guilty if you didn't."

"Yeah," I say. "She would just want me to be happy, though."

"She sounds like a lovely person," Zoe replies, and then, pointing to the front of the room with her eyes: "and looks it too."

"She was beautiful…" I say, trying to remember what she looked like as hard as I can. A picture can only do so much; I want to see how she looked in the mornings when she was having her first tea of the day. How she smiled when she designed a new bouquet. How she cried with me when I'd had my heart broken.

I wish I had known that I could hurt much worse. My breakup seems meaningless now that I've felt this kind of loss. Everything does.

"I bet it's hard, isn't it?" she says when I don't continue to talk. Usually, I'd belt out some sort of comeback like *of course it bloody is…* but I don't.

"Impossibly."

"It's a shame that everyone's come in black," she says. "It's not a funeral."

"That's what I was thinking," I say, giving a side eye to practically everyone in the room. "It's like they didn't know her at all and now they're remembering her wrong. She loved colour but she hated black; she said it was soulless."

"Was she quite passionate about it?" Zoe asks with a smile.

"Incredibly," I say. "She thought that colour made everything brighter and it made people smile."

"Well, maybe we need to bring a bit of colour to this event?" she suggests.

I raise my eyebrows and tilt my head, curious what she means by that.

"Is there a shop around here? One where we can get a few *supplies*?"

"Depends what 'supplies' they are," I laugh. "But the town centre is a ten minute walk from here. Do you think anyone would notice we've left?"

"So what if they do?" Zoe asks. "Surely you've got a free pass today?"

"Alright," I say, holding out my arm for her to link with. "Let's do some shopping."

The two of us are like peas in a pod as we rush from the building, giggling as we make our way into the car park. I swear I saw Debbie do a double take but she was so engaged in a conversation with a bald guy that she couldn't do anything about it. So, I guess we've got away with it, for now.

"So, I'm guessing you moved to our town because of your Mum dying?" Zoe asks. It's amazing how blunt she is with it; I hate when people try to dance around the point. It doesn't make it any easier for me. Why would it? I have to think about it more to figure out what they're attempting to say.

Besides, it's not like it can undo her death. She's gone, no matter how they try and hide it.

"Yeah," I answer her, seeing no reason not to. Zoe is the first person in a long time to actually care about how *I'm* feeling, rather than whether or not it's awkward for her. "My Dad just isn't in the picture; cliché, I know. So, I went to live with my grandma."

"Is she here today?"

"Nope," I say, a little bit of annoyance creeping through my words. "She only lives in the next town over; she's got no excuse not to be there."

"So, why isn't she?"

"She never really liked my Mum," I say. "Gran didn't say it explicitly but they were just so different to each other. They clashed a lot... It was kind of weird that I was sent to stay with her but she was the closest family member I guess. It would have been a bad idea to uproot the rest of my life too."

"But it happened anyway?"

"Yep," I explain. "She got her cancer diagnosis only two months after the accident and decided that was all she could handle. Which, to be fair, is a lot. But it felt more like a handy reason to get rid of me."

"That's not great," Zoe says. "Do you get on with your Auntie and Uncle? That's who you're with now, right? Brodie said you were cousins."

"You know Brodie?" Anyone who talks to that dork can't be that cool of a person... though, Zoe doesn't seem too bad yet.

"Not *well*," she says. "Please don't hate me but he's kind of weird."

"PAHAHAHA," I laugh. "As if I'd complain about that; he's a top notch douche. A* for being a pain in the frigging ass."

"You guys have a little sibling rivalry going on already?" she jokes.

"Far from it," I say seriously. "It's an actual, physical, *putrid* hatred. And somehow, everyone at school is like obsessed with him. I'm sure they'd get over it real quick after they caught a whiff of his bedroom."

"I do not need that visual," Zoe mocks.

"Hey; I only provided the smell," I say, throwing my hands in the air to play into my innocence. "It sucks, though. Whenever we're out in public together, people assume they're my brothers."

"It feels like they're rewriting your life?" Zoe asks and I look at her... *really* look at her.

"It sounds stupid, I know," I admit. "But I'm tired of it and it's not fair to Mum. She needs to be remembered correctly."

"Hence my plan!"

"Okay but what is this plan?" I ask. "You've been so cryptic about it all."

"You'll see soon enough," she smiles. "It will take your mind off everything, I promise. And it will drive your Aunt and Uncle crazy."

"Yeah, whatever it is, I'm down," I say.

"This looks like it will have what we need," she says, turning into the art shop. It's on the outskirts of town and is always one of the most deserted stores. People find it hard to be creative these days... there's always so much going on, so much to worry about. Green Haven isn't exactly where you live if you're 'comfortable' but the people here are incredible... so much better than my new home.

"What would we need from here?" I ask as we head in, hearing the ding of the bell above the door.

"Afternoon," the person at the desk says, tipping his hat forward.

"Hi," I say, rushing to catch up to Zoe. "What are you looking for?"

"Paint!" she says excitedly. "It needs colour... and we can bring it to them."

"You're a genius... but Debbie is going to ring my neck tomorrow!"

"Not today, though," she shrugs her shoulders. "We don't have to; it's your call. What would Eve want?"

I think about it, but it doesn't take long. Everyone else might have forgotten her but I haven't... I never will.

"Let's do it."

Four

Zoe and I buy a few different colours until we have a rainbow; I'm shocked when we hear how much it is at the till but it's a small price to pay to do this stupid event properly; to do Eve Myers justice.

"Everyone is going to be so confused," Zoe laughs as we head back. "*Oh no! My pretty dress! My shoes!*"

"*She must be so stricken with grief... how can we help her?*" I mock with her.

"This is gonna be absolutely brill!" Zoe says.

For a moment, life feels normal again... like the past year didn't happen. I used to laugh all the time like this with my old friends but once something happens to you that's this big, it's all people see when they look at you. I hate it so much; I just want people to look at me and think: that's Gracie. Is that too much to ask?

"You getting cold feet?" she asks, noticing my dropped mood.

"Not at all," I say. "Just thinking about things. I do a lot of that these days."

"I'm not surprised; I would do that too."

"I wish it was easier, you know? But that feels wrong too... like she wouldn't matter anymore," I explain, hoping it makes sense.

"So, a part of you still wants to be sad about it, because then it means you care?" she asks and I nod.

"Yep, that's about the gist of it," I confirm.

"I think that makes complete sense," she says simply. "I'd probably be the same. It's a tough situation, though; I don't think there's ever a *right* way to grieve. You just have to do your best. Like today... this event is just blatantly weird. We're going to make it better; make it mean something."

"Thanks, Zoe," I say, almost quietly. "No one else gets it."

"Maybe you just haven't given them a chance to," she suggests.

She has a point; I do tend to jump on people when they so much as open their mouth but I don't want to hear what they have to say. It's usually nothing worth hearing, anyway.

"You're very cryptically wise about all of this to say we've never spoken to each other before," I say, narrowing my eyes at her.

"I'm a good people watcher." She shrugs her shoulders, clearly not surprised at my having asked. "It's just what I do: try to help people."

And that's when I realise something. Zoe is a much better person than me. And I'm honestly just a pile of useless dog poo. I may have lost my Mum but I think I've been losing myself too... I've kind of noticed it, if I'm perfectly honest with myself, but I just don't want to admit it. It's like I have a vendetta against myself, paralysed in moments so I don't move on.

I can't.

I can't do that to *her*.

"Well, I guess it's now or never," she says as we trail into the car park.

I hate the fact that we're back already; I'd rather just play truant with Zoe for the afternoon, doing anything other than hanging around people I don't like. But I'm not doing this for me…

"Definitely now," I breathe, marching up to the front doors in my usual 'Gracie' fashion. I'm not letting these people steal my spunk so I can act like a sad and depressed orphan like they expect me to. I may not be okay with everything that happened but I'm not going to be soppy about it here of all places. Not where they can all see me.

Instead, I need to do what I do best: put on a damn good show and cause a little bit of havoc.

"Gracie?" Debbie says, trying to grab my arm as I storm in. But I shake her away, not looking away from the front of the room where all the wacky memorabilia is. Zoe strides after me, equally confident, and then we empty our 20p carrier bag of paint, cracking open the lids.

"Ready?" I say and Zoe gives me the biggest grin ever. It's like we're partners in crime… best friends for life… about to make a massive mess.

I open the first bottle of paint… purple. Standing on chairs in the front row, we begin to squirt it into the air, sending it flying onto flowers and walls and people.

This is for you, Mum. I'm bringing the colour back.

"Gracie!" Debbie is absolutely furious, her nostrils flaring more than ever. "Get down this instance!"

"Sorry, Auntie," I say slyly. "You guys are all depressing and honestly, it's just not a good look. But... purple would look great with your pantsuit!" I use the last of the bottle to douse her in colour, smiling at my creation. Her eyes glare at me through her new look, pools of neon dripping from her cheeks.

"You are in so much trouble." She's practically seething.

"That's class," Brodie laughs behind her, getting the whole thing on camera.

"Debbie, dear," some old woman says, patting her on the back. "It's a tough day for her; we all need to cut her some slack and understand how hard this is."

"There's only so many times I can 'cut her some slack'," Debbie says. "She's getting out of hand! It's been a year, for God's sake! She should be over it by now!"

What?

What did she say?

A year is barely any time at all... I lost my *Mum*. My best friend. And I lost her in an awful way; it was practically murder.

The bottle of paint drops from between my fingers, hitting the floor with a splat. But I don't care. I don't give any fucking shits anymore. Because I've had it with this stupid family. I've had it with *everyone*.

"She needs to grow up," Debbie says, as though she hasn't caused enough damage.

"*Me* grow up?" I say, shocked that she's even capable of being this horrible. "*Me?*"

"Yes, you!" she shouts back. The whole hall is silent now, listening to the problem child being told off; what a great fucking show for them all. "You're not the only one who lost someone, Gracie."

I try to think of something to say; some snarky comment about how she just doesn't get it. But I can't… she walks away, her heels clicking down the aisle between the chairs. Heads turn to watch her leave as Brodie lowers his phone.

Once again, I've ruined everything. It's all my fault. Because no matter how much I keep trying to refuse to believe it, something is wrong with me…

People loved me when Mum was alive. I was the delight of the town, a little kid always happy and doing the things she loves. But it all changed when she was killed; it's like they became scared of me, worried about what I'll do.

But I'm not going to do anything stupid… or dangerous. I just want to get through this and come out of it with some part of my integrity still intact. I think it might be a bit too late for that now.

"Forget it," I whisper. I don't know who I'm talking to; I don't even care anymore. None of these people matter.

"Are you okay?" Zoe asks me, looking all concerned. She looks just like everybody else; their eyes telling me that they think I'm a pitiful disaster.

"Oh, just fuck off," I say, stepping down from the chair and marching off too. I don't have to be here. I don't have to be here at all.

When I get to the car park, I see Debbie climbing into her car, crying into her hands.

I'm the one who should be upset. She's just being selfish, annoyed that she had to take me in on top of her own two children. Well, maybe I'll make it easier for her... run away, leave them all to it. It's not like they want me around anyway.

Debbie and Steve are always shouting at me; I can't do anything right. Brodie is more concerned about his own image than how I'm feeling... and Dexter doesn't care about anything unless it benefits him directly.

But I can't exactly do it now, can I? All of my things are back at Debbie's and I'm not going anywhere without them, especially since I saved some of Mum's things.

No, I can't run away now but I will.

I'm not staying in their shit hole of a town in that stupidly cramped house full of idiotic people. I don't even need them.

Five

The drive back is very awkward, but I bare it with my arms crossed and my lips pouted all the way home. I just have to keep the act going until tonight and then I can pack a bag and sneak away into the dark. Not that I have to pretend to be annoyed right now; I'm absolutely fuming with everyone.

"Gracie," Brodie whispers, nudging me softly.

I grimace at him, hoping he will regret getting my attention. But instead, he decides to continue talking.

"I need to show you something later."

"I don't want to see your dick pics," I say decidedly.

"No - no, it's not that," he says, glaring at the front seats. But who cares if his dear little Mummy and Daddy hear? Everyone in this house wouldn't be surprised if he had any. Maybe Dexter but he's a kid; he doesn't count. "It's something they should have showed you a long time ago."

His eyes dart softly back to the front seats as I think about what he's saying... basically that they've been lying to me about something, *keeping* something from me.

"Alright, fine," I say. "When?" I'm not particularly glad I have to find out from him but I hate people talking about me behind my back. And who knows what Debbie and Steve have got going on that they should have 'showed me a long time ago'? Like, what does that even mean? It's so cryptic.

"Midnight," he says. "In the attic."

Oh, this is just great. My Mum died a year ago today and he's wanting to organise secret meet ups in the middle of the night. I roll my eyes but there's no way I'm *not* going; annoying or not, he's got me intrigued.

He leaves it at that, somehow satisfied with my lack of an answer and heads back into the world of music. He always has his headphones on at home, never at school. No, there he's everyone's favourite person: the guy that every girl wants to date. To me, he's my stupid cousin who hogs the bathroom and forgets to put the toilet seat down.

He's nowhere near the worst in that damn house, though. No, right now, Debbie gets the award for the most awful and selfish human in existence. I hate her. I hate her. I hate her.

She will regret it later. When she wakes up in the morning, she will be shouting the house down, complaining that I haven't come down for breakfast. And then she will of course storm up to my room, throwing open my door and seeing my empty bed... then my empty wardrobe... then my shoes missing from the front door.

She will go absolutely crazy, especially when she realises it's all her fault.

It's such a great image to think about.

But where should I go? Maybe Zoe would let me stay at hers for a few nights but other than the fact that she's probably mad at me too, what good would going there do? It doesn't bring my old life back but can anything?

Maybe that's lost forever now, six feet under with Mum's bones.

"Right," Steve says, pulling into the driveway. "I think we should all have a talk before we go off."

Debbie glares at him, looking like an older version of me. Eww, no; why did I compare myself to that witch?

"I didn't do anything," Brodie says.

"Neither!" Dexter argues from his car seat.

"Thanks for the support guys," I add.

"Yeah, you're good by yourself," Brodie reminds me... and it's true. I've never needed anyone to fight my battles for me.

Last year was difficult; I'd practically watched my own Mum die in front of me but I'm getting through it. And I'm doing it without anyone's help. Sure, Debbie and Steve might have put a roof over my head but they haven't been here for me emotionally. The word 'therapy' hasn't even been floated about so they clearly don't think I'm worth it. Or maybe they just don't want to spend money or time getting me some actual help for the absolute mess of a year I've had.

But no.

None of that.

Sweet Gracie can deal with it all by herself.

But you know what? I have. Was I a blubbering mess today? Crying by her picture? Telling sob stories to anyone who would listen?

No, I damn well was not.

But am I okay? If I really think about what it means to be that, am I?

Maybe not. But I'm still alive... still living for her. I just wish it was *with* her.

"Just a little chat," Steve continues. As if he's going to win this fight; Debbie and I might hate each other but we still have the same fiery stubbornness.

"Fine," Debbie says. "But only if Gracie apologises."

"*Me?*" I stutter, disbelief flooding through me. I really can't believe that she's this heartless; actually, on second thought, I shouldn't be surprised.

She's always been distanced, even when Mum was alive. At every family event, she was always stood on the sidelines, judging everyone with her harsh glances. I never paid much attention, though; I was always too enthralled by everything else that was going on.

But as soon as we'd get home, I'd hear my Mum on the phone, complaining to somebody on the other end about her terrible sister.

Eve Myers would be turning in her grave if she knew I'd been dumped with Debbie. It's a good thing she'll never know.

As soon as the ignition is switched off, I climb out and slam the car door behind me. It's at this point that Brodie hands me a bag, hidden in his own.

"The paint," I whisper.

"Thought you'd want it," he shrugs, as though it's nothing. Not that it is...

I open up the bag and look at the tubes of colour. It seems like ages ago when Zoe and I had been to buy them but it was only a few hours ago. As usual, it's taken me no time at all to 'ruin' everything.

I follow after Brodie, thankful that Steve has already unlocked the front door. I begin to climb up the stairs, trudging muck on the carpet, when he calls me back down.

"Nice try," he says. "Everyone into the living room; you included, Brodie."

"So unfair," he moans but he heads in anyway. He's never really in a mood to argue or do anything exciting really.

I'm the complete opposite, always on a rampage of some kind, blasting my music and rattling the walls. But what else can they expect from me after everything I'd had to deal with? I've got the perfect hand-picked excuse to behave like this.

Besides, I hate silence.

"Can I go on the Xbox?" Dexter asks as Debbie ushers him into the living room.

I take a seat next to Brodie on the sofa and make myself comfortable; I have a feeling that this won't be a short talk that's done and over with. It never is with these people.

"Right," Steve begins. I think he's decided to mediate since Debbie has literal fumes protruding from her ears. He can mediate all he likes; I'm not apologising. "So, things got a bit out of hand over at Green Haven."

Debbie's bottom lip begins to quiver. God, she's so annoying. She must be putting it on; there's no way she can be this angry about some paint, especially since Mum would have loved it and this stupid event was for *her*.

"Gracie, you shouldn't have left," Steve continues, talking to me like I'm five. "And you shouldn't have behaved disrespectfully."

I don't think I did... right? Zoe and I were just trying to make it more colourful, make it match Mum's personality when she was alive. It was all in *her* name.

"You ruined it, Gracie," Debbie says, finally chiming in. "We spent months planning it and you just flounced in how you always do and wrecked everything."

"What happened to my 'get-out-of-jail-free' card?" I ask. "Huh?"

"What are you on about?" Steve asks.

"You guys have been fawning over me all week," I remind them. "I could do no wrong. You expected me to believe that I was suddenly a golden child? I know that you've been pitying me."

"We have not," Steve says but the lie is so blatantly obvious I could puke.

"You so have," Brodie adds. "We're not blind."

"I'm surprised you can see anything over that phone screen," Debbie says, looking at him with tears brewing in her eyes. Why does she have to be so dramatic?

"Let's all keep calm," Steve says and I fold my arms in response, laying back into the sofa cushions. "It was an emotional day, I get that; we *all* get that. But that doesn't give you the right to be rude or misbehave. Now, Gracie, I think you owe your Aunt an apology."

I glare at him, a moody vapour seeping from my eyes; does he think I'm stupid? Easily convinced? Hell no. Zoe and I were simply setting things right.

"I'm not going to do that," I say.

"Then, we will have to ground you," Steve says. "Until you say sorry."

"Then I guess I'll be grounded until I move out." Or, until I run away from this dump. So, in that sense, I guess it doesn't really matter.

"And you're really okay with that?" Debbie asks me. Her jaw is hanging down so much that if she was a cartoon character, it would be trailing on the floor.

"Why not?" I say sarcastically, kicking my feet onto the coffee table. "I just love hanging out here!"

"It is impolite to have your shoes on the table," Steve says, trying to keep himself calm. They're both seconds from blowing and I love it.

"It's impolite to be a jerk," I bite back, hoping to annoy them just a little bit more.

"Right," Steve says. He looks confused; did he really think I'd apologise that easily? It's Debbie who should be on her knees begging for my forgiveness. "Well, go to your room."

"Happily," I say, rising from the sofa. You don't need to tell me twice.

As I began my trudge upstairs, carrier bag of paint in hand, I think about how awful today has been. It seems so unfair and I am beyond annoyed at Debbie and Steve; I'm not surprised, though.

At least I can look forward to meeting Brodie at midnight. He's so bloody mysterious but it's something to turn my mind to... something to distract myself from the pain.

Six

Apparently, being grounded means I'm not allowed to come down for tea. See if I care, though. Family dinners are the worst thing; at least now I get to eat my fish fingers and potato waffles in peace.

Mum would be turning over in her grave if she could see me eating this processed rubbish. She was always raving on about how important your diet is, wanting to make sure I was healthy and lived a long life.

It didn't do her any good though, did it? She's now six feet under and the fact she always made sure to get her five a day didn't stop the car, did it?

No.

Someone still hit her.

Someone still killed my Mum.

I've spent months wondering who it was behind that wheel, trying to figure out who could be so heartless as to just keep on driving. They have to know what they did. You can't just send a body flying across the pavement, landing with a thump, legs and arms mangled.

Don't they feel guilty? I know I do. I wonder how different it could have been if she had been to walk down the street and make it onto the next.

Would've, could've. Should've.

But didn't.

I close my bedroom door behind me, throwing the bag of paints by my desk and laying on my bed. I hate this room; these four walls are a constant reminder that my life has changed and my home is no longer home.

I'll never be back in my childhood bedroom, being called downstairs by my Mum's voice. It can only exist as a memory now and I never even tried hard to remember it properly. It's just a blur. A forgotten part of who I was.

And who am I now? A complete nobody? The daughter of a dead woman?

It probably doesn't even matter. There isn't anything that I can do to change the path that I'm on; I became stuck here exactly one year ago today. And I don't think I actually want to leave it because it's not been long enough to finish mourning her. Maybe it never will be; isn't that a scary thought?

I waste the hours way waiting for Brodie by doing countless boring things. I spend a while reading my battered copy of *Call Me by Your Name* but eventually the fun wears away as my brain takes over...

Your Mum's dead. Your Mum's dead. Your Mum's dead.

So I place it face down on my bedside, saving my place with the receipt I'd used last time too. I've never been one for bookmarks. That would require some basic level of organisation and I've got zero.

But Eve was always so meticulous with things like that. She had all of her bookmarks stored neatly in these tiny little drawers in the corner of her bookcase, separated by colour or theme of something. I don't quite remember but she loved to read. At least we have that in common...

Eventually, I check my phone. I've been avoiding it for hours, scared to see the lack of notifications on my lock-screen. But it's not completely empty:

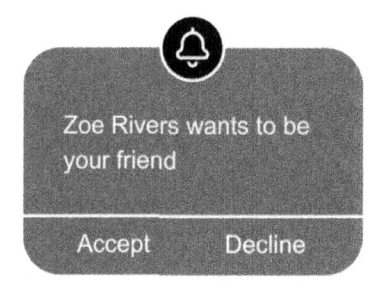

> 🔔
> Zoe Rivers wants to be your friend
>
> Accept   Decline

Hmm. Interesting development.

I click onto it, opening up my social media. There isn't any real harm in accepting, unless of course she wants to complain at me about earlier. She'll have to join the queue, though.

Without anymore hesitation, I press on the little 'accept' button, hoping it won't be a bad idea. I don't like the idea of having friends but maybe it would be good to have someone around at school.

It's always so quiet, walking through the bustling corridors by myself to eat my lunch in a deserted corridor.

I'm perfectly prepared for that to be all I'll ever have and so, when my phone screen lights up on my blanket, I'm a little surprised.

> Hey, I hope you're feeling a bit better about everything.

> Today must be really tough but it was fun adding a bit of colour!

I'm not sure why she's so bothered about how I am. It's not like I've given her any reason to care or like me, especially after earlier. But I don't entirely mind her being there, sending a lovely message while I'm feeling like this...

> It's a shame Debbie went and ruined it all :/

I'll never pass up an opportunity to complain about my Aunt and I definitely won't today of all days. She opens my message straight away, three little dots appearing almost instantaneously.

> Your aunt is so uptight! Hope everything's okay back home though!

It sounds like a ploy... like another nosy parker trying to find out if I'm okay and how I'm handling it all. So, why do I reply?

> It's a bloody shambles.

> Been grounded too!

> That's so unfair! Wanna do something tonight? We can sneak you out.

> I so would but Brodie has something he needs to show me.

> He asked to meet me at midnight !!

> That's a bit cryptic!

> Tell me about it.

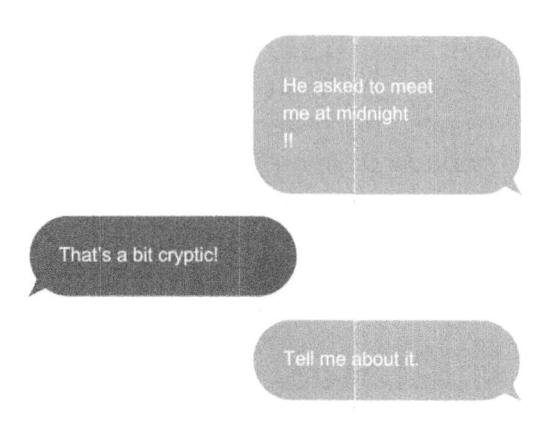

As soon as I send the message, I regret it.

I don't know Zoe and that in itself is weird. But I don't talk to people in general, not about private things, not about my Mum. People never mean what they say; I've come to learn that. They pester you, trying to make sure you appear okay, but they don't really care about how you feel on the inside. They don't realise that my whole life has turned upside down and I've got nothing left to live for.

But I'm still here. I'm still trying for her.

It's not long until midnight now... there are only so many minutes left of waiting around like a wet wipe for my stupid cousin. Whatever he wants to show me, it better be good. I don't know what I'll do it isn't; I can't really do anything, can I? I'm already in enough trouble as it is. But I can just check what it is and then my plan of running away can resume. Because I'm still doing it, I think. Why wouldn't I? There isn't anything for me here, in this rundown seaside town, with these awful people who don't give two hoots about me.

I shuffle into my slippers, not wanting to brave the coldness that exists outside of my bed sheets. Debbie literally refuses to have the heating on, even though it's absolutely freezing at this time of year. She's always going on about how to save money, not that they need to. Their house is huge in comparison to the terraced home I used to live in with Mum. But there isn't any money in the florist business… Being a finance manager on the other hand? Let's just say, Debbie's job only exists to buy her a nice home with a double garage and a swimming pool in the back.

It was never about the money for Eve Myers, though. We were never uncomfortable but we didn't have anything to spare. There were important things to life, that's what she said. I don't know if I believe all that now; you can do a lot of things if you have money. Like running away and starting again somewhere else. Like trying to plaster over an absence of a person that can never come back.

Throwing my dressing gown around my body, I take my phone again to use as a torch, shining a path of light along my carpet to the door. It usually creaks but there is a knack to doing it quietly, avoiding being caught by prying adults with nothing better to do.

Brodie is already waiting for me by the door that hides the stairs to the attic. Of course, they wouldn't have a ladder to access it like most normal houses but I suppose it's a good thing in this situation; there is no way you can pull one of those down without making a noise.

"You're late," he whispers.

"I'm here, aren't I?" I say, though I think I'm actually bang on time so I don't know why he's complaining.

"Let's just go up," he replies, twisting the knob slowly and beginning to tiptoe up the winding staircase. I follow him, closing it just as softly behind me and dousing us in darkness.

Seven

Once we reach the top of the steps, Brodie flicks the light switch on, revealing the two sofas and scatter of beanbags him and his friends usually all hang out on. I've always told him that he needs to have fairy lights to achieve the ultimate vibes but he always says the other guys would laugh at it. It's really not my problem if his mates are big wieners.

But I'm grateful that they at least have seating as I lounge back into one of the sofas, curling up under a throw blanket.

"Right, what do you need to show me?" I ask, ready to get this moving along fast. "Aren't you going to sit down?" I add, realising that he's hovering by the door still.

"One moment," he replies, heading over to the entrance to the cupboard in the eaves of the house. Once he opens it, a musty smell creeps into the air. He pulls out a box that's been squished in, bent in the middle from the pressure. It's a little dusty but I'm not surprised; things get thrown in there all the time and forgotten about.

He closes the cupboard and heads over to sit beside me, resting the box on his lap.

"What's that?" I ask, annoyed at how coy he's been. Why can't he just say it and get it over with? Why is he turning it into this massive thing?

"It belonged to your Mum," he says.

Okay, so maybe that's why it's taken him so long. Fair enough.

"Not the box itself but the things in it. My parents found it not long after it happened, when they were clearing out the house."

The reminder hits me harshly, images of the flurry of cardboard boxes piled with her belongings... the things we both used in our daily routines. Gone. Packed away. Sent to charity shops and handed out to relatives.

"They thought it would be bad timing to give it to you so soon after everything," he continues. "So, they put it in here and hid it."

"They can't care that much if that's the state it's in now," I complain. But I don't care about them at this point. I just *have* to know what's in there, what's been left behind.

"Look, do you want it or not?" he asks, balancing it in his hands in front of me. I stare at it, my eyes dropping to the crease along the top. I'm absolutely terrified to take it for some reason but I can't look like a dunce in front of Brodie; he needs to know that I'm tough. Unphased. Fine.

And so I take it.

It's not heavy... am I disappointed? I think so. I don't know, though. I should just be grateful for any part of her.

"Did you open it?" I ask him.

"Yeah," he admits. "I didn't know what it was. The boys and I were looking for some of our old games and I came across it. I didn't recognise it so I just had a peek."

"They didn't see it too, did they?" I ask him. Brodie seeing my Mum's things is one thing but his friends doing it would be invasive, strange.

"No, I'm not that bad," he says, looking at me as though I shouldn't even be questioning it at all.

But it's not like I know him well. We were never close as children, our parents living in separate towns and not really liking each other. I guess in that sense, it's kind of ironic that I ended up here of all places... the original plan was to be with my grandma but obviously that went a little tits up. But it doesn't matter, either place is shit compared to my real home... somewhere I can never go back to.

"Thank you," I say. I'm kind of grateful he kept it to himself, shocked too. I look down at the box shaking softly between my fingers. It feels scary to have it here, the unknown lurking between my two hands like it could change everything. Maybe it could? Or maybe, and most probably, it's just a pile of collected junk. I don't think Debbie and Steve would have rifled through everything and actually thought about what would have been important to my Mum. They wouldn't even know if they did.

I take the lid off, placing it by my feet. There are a few random items in there... a lighter she used to get the hob working, a small teddy she won me at the amusements in town... a notebook?

It's the biggest thing in there, so maybe that's why I'm intrigued by it the most. But no matter the reason, I take it out, opening it to the first page:

EVE MYERS' DIARY

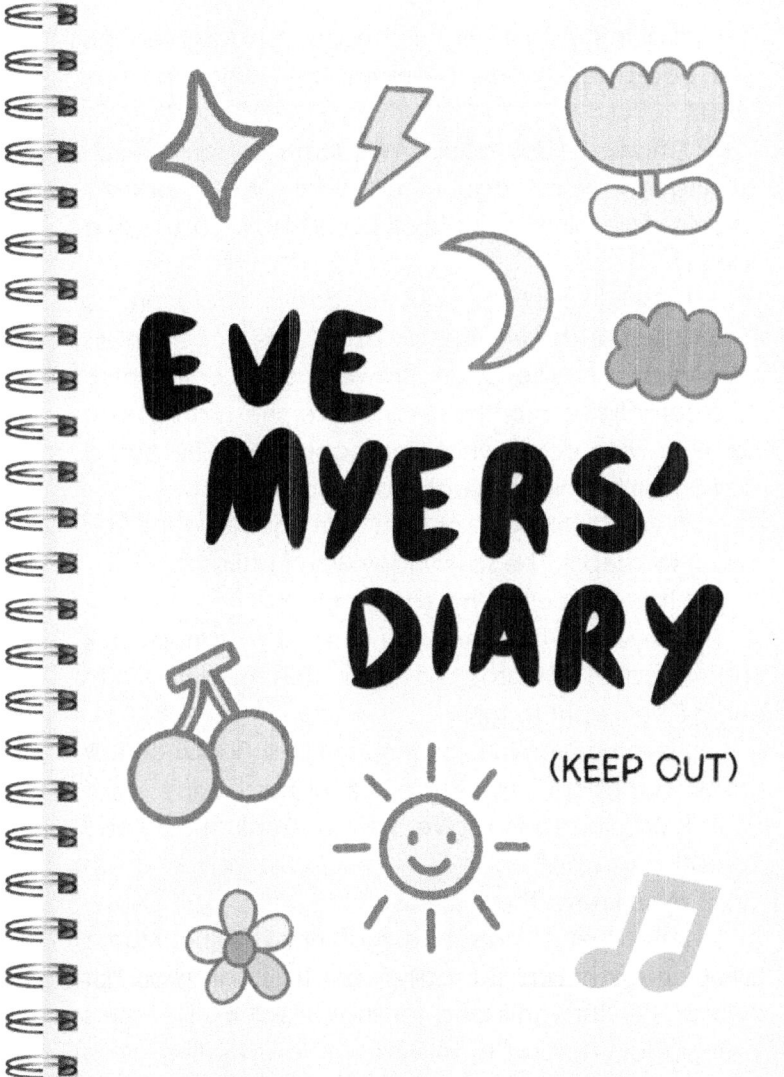

(KEEP OUT)

"I didn't read it," Brodie begins. "But I did see the first page. That's how I remembered what the box was."

"Thanks," I say again. Why am I just on repeat, saying my words again and again like a parrot? Brodie must think I'm an idiot, paralysed because of a box.

I start to flick through the pages. There are so many words here, the dates at the top corners spanning numerous years. Between each entry, there are sometimes months missing, like she didn't have time to write down what had happened. She had a kid and a business, though; I don't blame her.

"I won't tell Mum or Dad that you have it if you want to keep it," he says. "They won't notice."

"Thanks," comes my same reply.

"Anyways, I'll leave you to it." He stands back up, heading towards the door nonchalantly. "I'm here if you want to talk."

I'd rather vomit all over myself at school than talk to Brodie about anything personal but I don't say it out loud. Instead, I give him a small smile, and breathe in relief once he's gone. Or maybe it's in fear. Who knows these days?

But all that matters is that I'm holding Mum's diary in my hands. If I really want to, I can read her words, her thoughts and feelings. It will be like she's here again, talking to me like we're updating each other after I get back in from school.

Yet, thinking this way makes the silence around me heavier than it should be.

I have two choices here: a decision to make.

I can read my Mum's diary and feel closer to her. Or, I can respect her privacy and put it back away in the box, hiding it in the attic cupboard again.

But I suppose there is a third option: I can take it with me, keep it close. Yes, that's much better.

So why am I opening to the first entry?

13th June 2001

Dear Diary,

I have never kept one of these things before but everything is changing and I want to write it down, have some way to remember it all when I'm older and my memory has faded. I've never had much to live for but I think I do now.

I met someone!

Can you believe it?

He had been at my sixth form for a little bit of our first year but decided to drop out and head into full time work at his Dad's garage instead: *Grayson's*. And so, I suppose I've known him for quite a few months now, only I haven't seen him again until recently. And by recently, I literally mean last weekend!

So, I was heading back from my last class of the day and I'd decided to go to the garage to see if they had any cheap cars for sale. I've wanted to learn for ages and now that I've finally turned seventeen, it's becoming an option. But my parents refuse to buy me a car; they say I need to work hard to earn my own things. I think they're just trying to encourage Debbie and I to be good people and my sister revels in it.

But I don't want my whole life to be about chasing money… I want to be happy. Loved. That's it, really, that's all I want.

And maybe I will be soon!

The garage I went to just so happens to be the one he works at! I recognised him straight away, his mullet and low-rise jeans just as unfashionable as they had been before. But that smile - that damn smile…

He couldn't remember who I was at first and I don't really blame him. I'm not exactly quiet at school anymore but, in those first few months, I was nervous and timid, trying to find friends without embarrassing myself.

But I gave him a reminder and he was super excited to see me here. We ended up having a bit of a conversation about what we've both been up to... it seems he's been doing a lot.

I feel behind as a teenager, realising all the things I'm missing out on because of my parents.

I don't know what I did to impress him but when I had to leave to head home for dinner, he asked if I wanted to hang out this Friday night. That's literally tomorrow now...

Of course, I said yes! Why wouldn't I?

I've never had a boyfriend before and, to be fair, if Mum and Dad find out, they will literally kill me. They'd never get over it but I think if I let him know that, he will be okay with it. He seems to be a guy who understands things and I need someone like that in my life so badly.

So, I guess I'll have to let you know how it goes tomorrow!

If I'm honest... I've walked past the garage on the way back from sixth form every day since, *hoping to catch a glimpse of him, a smile through the window!*

Anyways, got to go but wish me luck!

Eve

Who is this about? My Dad?

I've never known him; he'd left before I had even been born and Mum had never really said why. But the dates line up... she had me when she was newly eighteen, young and alone. But his identity was always kept a secret.

"You're better off not knowing," she would always say.

I gave up asking years ago, realising that there wasn't much point if I'd get no response.

But I wanted to know who he was, I still do. And maybe the answers are in this diary? All I have to do is keep reading and I could know everything, even the things she didn't want me to. I have a choice here but I know that there's only really one outcome.

I put the notebook back in the box, placing the squished lid on top. It feels too light; is this really all I have left of her? And, as I tuck it under my arm and head back down the attic stairs, I cry for the first time in months.

Eight

I replay my Mum's words all night long, turning over in my bed as I picture the garage and this mysterious man she had fancied back when she was younger. You'd think it would be hard without all the details but my brain fills in the empty spaces for me, creating a lifetime of memories and flashing them across my mind in a story graph.

When I see the sun creeping through the gaps in my curtains, I groan, realising that I really did not get much sleep at all. I thought that things would get easier. She died a year ago now and each day was supposed to get a tiny bit better until time had healed all wounds, or whatever it is people say. So why do I feel like absolute hell? Why does it still hurt like it happened yesterday?

I don't know how people do this, how they carry on with their lives as though that person never existed in the first place, how they fill their absence. I can't do it. I *won't* do it. Because then that means I've forgotten her, right? And I don't want that to ever happen; it would be so much worse.

So I tumble from my bed sheets and head into the bathroom to wash away the fragments of yesterday that keep spilling into my brain. Besides, I didn't have a shower yesterday and I don't need to add to my problems by turning up at school stinking of B.O. Teenagers are ruthless but even more so when no one cares about you because then you're an easy target. Not even my own cousin wants to associate himself with me and I can't even blame him; how sad is that?

But the running of the water isn't loud enough to block out my thoughts. Instead, they slither into the crevices and, as I wash my body, I'm crying all over again. It seems impossible that I'll be able to make it through the whole day, especially now that I have Mum's diary. But the chances of Debbie and Steve letting me stay home are slim to none but it's worth a try.

I dry myself off and change into my school uniform, grimacing as I fasten my tie around my neck. It's suffocating, locking itself against my skin and sending hot flashes across my face. At least I look the part to try and skive school.

"Debbie," I say, tiptoeing into the kitchen and clutching my stomach. "I'm not feeling well."

She stares at me, not even pausing her cooking. I don't know how she's able to flip the bacon without seeing it; it's honestly kind of creepy.

"Can I skip school today?" I ask, realising she isn't going to answer me.

"No," she says bluntly. "You can get on with life like everyone else."

"But I'm ill?" I question, holding onto my tummy to really sell it.

"And I'm Bill Gates," she replies. She's not even looking at me anymore, clearly giving up on the idea of indulging me before she could begin.

"Ugh," I complain, turning on my heels. There's no point sticking around for breakfast here; I'll grab something on the way. Instead, I head back up to pack my bag, placing Mum's diary carefully in the laptop pocket. My books always get absolutely wrecked when I put them in there, so I'm hoping that it will be okay. Either way, I can't leave it here for Debbie or Steve to find. Besides, I want to be close to her and carrying around her words will help with that. It's almost as though I'll be able to talk to her whenever I read it; I know that it sounds stupid. It is a little bit but it's all I have.

I might tell Zoe about it, update her on what went on after I met Brodie last night. She probably deserves to be included after how she helped me at the memorial service. But I'll think about it and decide in the moment. For all I know, she's decided that it's too much hassle to be friends with someone like me, someone with so much trauma and baggage attached to her. I'm only sixteen and I've known the worst tragedy.

It's pathetic, really.

But there she is, stood at the end of my street just as I'm about to round the corner.

"Did we make plans?" I ask, though I know for a fact that we didn't. I stop in my tracks before I get too close to her; I don't want it to look like I'm with her, like I've accepted the fact that she's been waiting here to walk in with me.

"No," she says, a small grin forming on her lips. "But I thought you'd want to walk in together."

"And you couldn't text me because?" I question further.

"I did," she answers bluntly. "Someone didn't reply."

I feel the heaviness of my phone in my pocket all of a sudden. I've barely checked it, that's true; I've been preoccupied, though.

"So, shall we head in?" Zoe asks.

I freeze, thinking hard.

Since Mum died, the idea of having friends is truly terrifying and I don't even know why... I should want people to talk to, people to rely on to help me through this. But it makes me feel sick, being close with someone again. But Zoe doesn't have to be a *real* friend; she can just make school a little easier to bear.

"Okay," I agree, beginning to walk down the street again. She follows after me without hesitation. "But I need to get some breakfast on the way."

"They don't feed you in there?" she jokes.

"Nothing edible," I bite back.

"Well, there's a Bakery near to the school gates," Zoe says, bringing the seriousness back. "We can head there and I can buy a coffee then. I'm exhausted."

"Didn't you sleep?"

"Not really," she says. "I struggle sometimes. I'm probably an insomniac."

"Haven't you been to the doctors about it?" I ask, genuinely curious.

"What's the point? They will just tell me that I need to sleep more or something else that's equally useless."

I guess it's true; the hospital did nothing for my Mum. I had to watch her die, all hooked up to their futile machines as she breathed her last moment. She should have been saved… she was alive when she was brought there, even if barely, so there was a chance! But no one did anything; they let her die.

I watched my own Mum die.

And I'll never not be angry about that.

We arrive at the bakery soon enough and, I recognise the old, chipped building straight away. I must have walked past it countless times in the past year that I've lived here, only to never really look at it, never take it in. It looks like the rest of this town, though; a little bit worn around the edges. A true Yorkshire shop.

Zoe heads straight in, a small bell chiming above my head as I follow after her. Inside, it's very cosy, with fairy lights strung against the walls and peaceful art dotted around.

"I come here all the time," Zoe smiles, joining the back of the queue.

There's only one other person in front of us and they are in the same school uniform as us. I don't recognise them, though, even though they look our age.

"Do you know what you want?"

I look at the coffee options plastered on the menu boards. I don't know why I bother, though; I always get the exact same one in memory of her: a gingerbread latte. She loved all things Christmas, so whenever she could spread it throughout the year, she would. Turns out, that can be done through a simple coffee syrup.

But the food? I can't just have a drink for breakfast, no matter how tempting it is. There are so many options in the glass counter that it's actually difficult to pick, especially with Zoe standing right there. I go for a safe option in the end, asking for a danish when it's our turn to order.

"Let me," Zoe says, cutting in with her arm to hand the barista some coins.

"Thanks," I say. Now that the transaction is done, I don't really have a choice.

The barista makes our coffees quickly enough and places a danish into a bag, passing them all over within just two minutes. I take the bag and my gingerbread latte, handing Zoe her mocha, and then we head back out into the air.

"Why did you do that?" I ask her, needing to know why she felt entitled to pay for me. It was probably pity; that's always what it is. Poor little Gracie - orphaned at fifteen. Except I'm not really completely parent-less; somewhere out there is a man who is my father. Maybe only biologically but that's got to count for something... perhaps Mum's diary holds the clue as to who he is. Her first entry talks about a boy who invited her on a date; he could be the one. I can find my Dad... tell him everything that has happened... tell him that I *need* him.

"To apologise for yesterday," she says, waking me from my thoughts.

I'm finished thinking about it all but I don't think that it's something I'm going to forget about easily. I can pick it back up later; for now, I want to know what on earth Zoe is on about.

"I just wanted to help make the memorial more - I don't know - real? Instead, you were grounded! Fat load of help, I was!"

"You didn't mean to," I say, batting the apology away. "I'm glad we did it. I just wish we could have decorated the room with a bit more paint before we had to stop." I add this last bit with a cheeky smile, thinking back to the paint bottles in my room.

"We can always brighten something else up," she shrugs.

"Like Debbie's car?" I suggest, thinking with satisfaction of the face my Auntie would pull when she saw it.

"I don't think you'd ever live that one down!" she laughs.

But before I can reply, I stop in my tracks.

"What? What is it?"

"Grayson's."

Nine

The name of the garage blurs more the longer that I stare at it, the letters dancing across the sign. There's no way it's here, the same one that Mum referenced in the diary. I thought she grew up in Green Haven for starters, not this shit hole.

I squat down on the pavement, placing my coffee cup and danish bag across the curb. Scrambling with the zip, I finally undo the bag and slide her diary out, turning to that opening page...

He had been at my sixth form for a little bit of our first year but decided to drop out and head into full time work at his Dad's garage instead: Grayson's.

It's the same name, that's for sure and certain. But why is it *here*? Why isn't it in the town that she said she'd always lived in?

"Gracie?" Zoe says, looking at me in confusion.

I might as well tell her now; she's already seen me lose my absolute mind multiple times in just twenty-four hours and I don't think she'll tell anyone. She better not, anyway.

"Can you keep a secret?" I ask, still practically sat on the ground.

"Of course," she answers, sitting down next to me. Realising I'm about to explain everything, I sit down properly too, cross-legged beside her, holding the diary in my lap.

"Brodie found some of my Mum's things," I say. "One of them was this."

She peers at the words on the first page.

"Her diary?"

"Yep," I breathe out. "I've only read the first entry."

"That's what he needed to show you last night," she says. It's all clicking together for her, just like it is for me too.

"Yeah," I say. "And look, it says that this boy she had a crush on worked at a garage called Grayson's, like that garage right there."

"I don't get it."

"Mum lied about living here," I explain. "She used to tell me all these stories about living in Green Haven, yet she was here... walking to the same school we're about to go to most likely."

"How do you know?"

"Because it says right here!" I point down at the page, showing her how she would walk past the garage after sixth form. "Our school has one; I see them all walking about without a uniform, thinking they're all cool because of it."

"They *are* cool," she laughs. "But go on."

"The garage has the same name that it did in 2001," I say, this time more slowly. There is so much importance in what I'm about to tell her, so much possibility. "I think it might belong to my Dad."

"What?" she says.

"Right, let me get you up to speed," I say, giving her a brief overview of how I've never known my Dad, how Mum would dance around my questions about him until I stopped asking altogether, how I never thought I *would* know him. "So, if the name is the same…"

"Then your Dad might own it by now…" she finishes. I nod my head, almost scared to admit it out loud. "Well, how do you know the guy from the garage is your Dad? You haven't read anything else yet. Maybe you should look at some more entries before you get your hopes up?"

"Too late," I say, biting my lip as I look over at the garage again. "I could just pop in?"

"And say what?" she asks.

"I don't know! Ask about car parts or something."

"You're sixteen," she reminds me. I roll my eyes at her.

"Are you coming or what?" I ask, putting Mum's diary back into the bag and tucking my danish beside it and gripping my gingerbread latte again. It sounds silly but I can really feel her with me and I am so damn glad because I am absolutely petrified.

We walk up to it, my steps slowing down the closer we get. It's scarier now that we're right beside it. It's feeling a little too real.

"We don't have to do this now, you know?" Zoe says.

But I want to so bad... why can't I do it? Why can't I walk into a stupid garage?

"Later," I say. "We need to get to school."

And I storm down the street... away from Grayson's... away from answers... away from Mum.

...

I spend my lessons drifting through the day, my mind skirting on the verge of everything that it *should* be focusing on. Exams are right around the corner but they seem useless now, insignificant compared to life. I can worry about them later, further on into year eleven. All I want to do right now is think about my Mum, to mourn her how I should be doing so that she's never forgotten. Because nobody else is remembering her *properly*... she's become someone who used to be here but is just a body now... six feet under in Green Haven's graveyard.

See, exams mean nothing in the grand scheme of things. It's people who I should care about; only certain ones, of course. For example, Debbie and Steve are perched on the top of the list of those I actually despise; it's a no mercy kind of hate.

And so, when I'm leaving the school gates and Zoe is once again waiting for me, my stomach fills with confusion. I don't get why she's attached herself to me all of a sudden; it's got to be pity. What else can it be?

"What do you want?" I ask, not stopping in my tracks as I begin to walk towards Debbie and Steve's house.

"I thought we could give the garage another crack," she says. Zoe follows after me like a lost little pup, except she's not as cute. There's a blandness about her, like she can't exist by herself or else she'd be too boring, nothing going on.

"And what if I don't want to?" I say back.

"I think you do," she says. "Deep inside, part of you needs this, right?" She says it so nonchalantly, like she's known me forever and can read me like a book.

"Fine!" I shout, turning around quickly to face her. "I want to, okay? But I also *don't* want to. I don't understand any of it and you going on about it isn't going to help."

"Okay..." she says softly, standing close to me. "Maybe we won't go today, then."

"We?" I raise an eyebrow but a little bit of me softens at the idea.

"We're in this together," she says. "As friends."

"Friends?"

"If you'll have me," she bobbles her head excitedly, shrugging her shoulders. She's determined,

I'll give her that. I suppose it's not a terrible idea; I could do much worse as far as friends go and she does seem to genuinely care which is rare around here.

"Okay," I say.

"Okay?" she smiles, clearly proud of herself as she adds, pointing at me playfully: "I can see that little grin there!"

"Oh, shush," I reply, desperate to change the subject. "So, Grayson's."

"Grayson's," she repeats. "We don't have to go today if you're not ready but maybe we could read the next entry? Or, you can. I won't look if you don't want me to."

"We can read it," I say, nodding to myself. It's me who needs convincing; the anxiety in my stomach is curling its way around again as I'm thinking about it all.

"Why don't we go to my house?" she suggests. I'm about to agree when I remember something.

"Ugh," I groan. "I'm grounded still, probably for the rest of my life at this point."

"Okay, so how about you sneak me into yours?" she says with a grin.

"I'm starting to think you've got a bit of a bad streak," I tell her.

"Only for things that are important."

"Okay, smart arse," I say. "I hope you're good at climbing."

Ten

I walk into Debbie and Steve's house alone, Zoe waiting awkwardly in the bushes at the side of the building underneath my bedroom window.

"I'm home!" I shout, bounding up the stairs in my shoes. I could care less about getting mud all over their immaculate carpet; Debbie and Steve deserve it. Luckily, I don't hear any response, be it words or footsteps behind me, and so I can close my bedroom door and not worry about being followed. After placing my bag on the carpet and sliding my Docs from my feet, I head on over to the window, peering down at Zoe stood far below. She's clocked already which glass pane is mine; there is only one other window upstairs along this side of the house and it clearly belongs to the bathroom. And so I turn the handle and push it open, meeting her gaze.

"How do I climb up?" she asks, perhaps a little too loudly.

I point down at the trellis that runs up this side of the building. It's filled with plants and hints of flower; Debbie hires a gardener to come take care of everything twice a month so that it can look presentable to the neighbours. She will go ballistic if Zoe messes them up but luckily I've left my own trail among the wood that she can follow.

Her face screams that I'm the crazy one, though, when she realises what I mean. Within a moment, she's flashing her hand across her throat as if to say 'no way' but I use my own hands to tell her to 'come on'. She shakes her head, assessing the trellis.

And she places a foot on the bottom, hoisting herself up step by step. She shockingly makes it look easy, especially since this is her first time. I've been up and down that thing on a few occasions now, escaping whenever I can to be by myself, and even I still struggle in a few places. But she's quick to get to the top and, before I know it, I'm helping her climb through the window and land safely in my room.

"How did you do that so well?" I ask her. I don't know whether to be annoyed from jealousy or just dead impressed.

"I've got my talents," she shrugs.

"I see that," I say, raising an eyebrow curiously. "Come on."

Closing the window again, I pick up my school bag and perch on the bed, waving Zoe over with my head to join me. She flicks off her shoes and sits cross-legged against the headboard, filling me with a strange sort of feeling. It's normal: this whole scene is completely mundane. But it feels new. No, not new; *forgotten*. I used to have friends over all the time when I was younger, spending countless weekends hanging out with the girls in my class. Mum would always bring in snacks for us but leave us to it; she knew it wasn't cool to hover.

Days like that don't happen anymore. Or, at least, they *didn't*, until now.

"So, do you want to read the next entry?" Zoe prompts me.

I nod my head in response, taking a breath before releasing the notebook from my bag's pocket. It feels heavy in my hand, now. Purposeful. Important.

"It's okay," Zoe whispers. "Take your time."

We could sit here for hours in silence, simply waiting to open to the next page. But I can't keep waiting; I need answers. I need to know.

5th June 2001

Dear Diary,

It went amazing! I can't quite believe it. Okay, let me tell you what happened properly, starting at the very beginning.

After school, I headed home quickly to get ready. I curled my hair... did my makeup... put on something special underneath my dress just in case. I don't think I've ever looked so beautiful and he seemed to think so too. From the moment we locked eyes, I think he wanted to kiss me. Granted, his face was a little foggy through the car window but he unrolled it, giving me the most handsome smile.

"Get in, then," he'd said. I was all giddy inside as I climbed into the passenger seat but I calmed myself down before he could see me. He's one of those cool kinds of guys, the ones who don't usually give girls like me a chance. So I have to really try to meet his standards so that he won't get bored of me.

He didn't even look at me before driving away from my street. All I can say is that I'm glad my parents were still at work because his car was making strange noises the whole way. It's a little ironic that it's in such bad nic when his family owns a garage.

He ended up taking me to the nearby forest. It's on the outskirts of town and faces out over the cliffs. I've been there a few times with friends, looking out at the sea and thinking about life. But it was different this time.

We parked up close by and walked in, traipsing between the trees. Unfortunately, it's warm this time of the year. Otherwise, I could have asked for his jacket. But there was no jacket and no cold, so I knew I'd have to show my interest in some other way.

He kept leading me deeper and deeper. Perhaps I should have been worried but I wasn't at all. I knew where he was taking me; a small clearing on the edge of the cliff where everyone hangs out. I've taken the path so many times that I know it more than the back of my hand.

When we finally got there, he laid his jacket out across the grass.

"Please," he said softly and I tucked myself on it, trying my best to remain decent despite my dress. Dad hated it when I spent my pocket money on it; he said it was far too short, too much. But I thought the floral pattern was actually mature and I've seen worse. Yet then, in that moment with him, I could feel his gaze dance along my legs. I wasn't sure how to feel. Wasn't this what I wanted? And I guess I still do... My friends will go crazy when they find out but he says I have to keep it between us two for now, just until he's sure. I agreed easily, knowing it will help to hide from my parents because no one else will know.

From here, we spent a little while talking. It was mainly about sixth form and Grayson's; his future there. I listened for ages, just watching his lips move, but eventually he grew tired of the talking. His hand clasped the side of my face and his eyes stared down at me almost aimlessly. I really thought I wanted to kiss him there and then but as his lips came close, I freaked out, pulling my face away.

"What's wrong?" he whispered.

"Sorry," I'd stumbled. "I'm sorry. I can't."

He didn't seem completely annoyed. Maybe a little disappointed, though. But I suppose I had led him on a little bit; he has every right to be angry. In the moment, I just couldn't go through with it...

He asked what was wrong but what if it's me? What if I'm the problem?

Eve

As I finish reading, I let the notebook rest against my legs, looking slowly up at Zoe.

"That doesn't sound like it went well to me," Zoe says.

"No," I reply, shaking my head softly. I don't know who the boy is in the entry. I don't even know what happened after. But there's a sickly feeling in my stomach as I think about how she must have felt at the time. My Mum was always so positive, so light, so happy, never holding onto the past. Yet, she must have felt so pressured to impress him so that he would stay. They might not have kissed on the fifth June but who's to say it ended there? The entry didn't mention anything about a second date but there are countless pages here, spanning the important things that happened since that time. And that's when I realise something: "She started this diary because of him."

"What do you mean?"

"The first thing she spoke about was this boy," I say, thinking out loud. "And it's all she's spoken about since. Whoever he is, he must be important because she started this diary because of him and then continued to write in it for…" I flip to the last page, scanning the date. "Sixteen years…"

"You mean…"

"Yeah," I say slowly. "Until she died."

Eleven

It feels weirdly morbid knowing that she's been keeping this notebook and writing down her memories and thoughts my whole life. It's even worse to think about why she's no longer adding to it.

"Okay," Zoe says, processing the information. "So, now we have two places we can visit: Grayson's and the forest."

"What I don't get is why she lied about growing up in Green Haven when she was here all along," I say. It hurts to think that she didn't tell me the truth; I thought we were closer than that.

"Something must have happened," Zoe suggests. "Maybe the answer is in the diary."

"Probably," I shrug.

"So, do you want to go to either of them?" she asks me. Her eyes look so concerned, drooping. It still doesn't make sense to me why she's trying so hard to befriend me; I haven't exactly made it easy for her.

"I'm grounded, remember?"

"Well, we can sneak out at lunch tomorrow," she says, as though it's nothing. Zoe always looks so innocent but the more I hang out with her, the more I'm realising that this isn't the case. There's a certain spunk to her that I can appreciate, as though I'm looking in the mirror at the girl I was before all of this. I honestly think I've mellowed out, lost touch with myself, traded in the things I loved to be a shell of memories.

"How would we do that?" I ask, unsure of how we'd even manage it. But then I think about it: this is something I would have done in the time before, back when I didn't have any cares in my way. I'd just jump. "You know what, let's do it."

"Really?" Zoe asks. There's a little hint of surprise slapped across her face and I'm glad of it. I'm so tired of people constantly pitying me, thinking that I'm less able to do things because my Mum died. Well, whoopdedoo, I'm still here. I'm still living. I'm still never forgetting her.

"Yeah, whatever," I reply as casually as I can. "We should head to the garage first; we might get more out of it than a bunch of trees."

"Well, it's more than that," she argues. "It's a way for you to connect with her again; it could be healthy for you, healing maybe."

"I'm not trying to heal, Zoe," I warn her. "That means I have to leave her behind and I can't do that."

"There are other ways to move on that doing it like that," she says.

"And what would you know about it?" I ask her, perhaps a little too harshly. "You don't know what it's like, that's all I mean. No one does and I'm sick and tired of everyone pretending they know how any of this feels."

"They're only acting like that because they don't get it," she explains. "Only you know what this loss feels like; they're just trying to navigate it all in the only way they know how. That means that they might not be doing it how you need them to but they *are* trying."

"Well, they can stop," I say.

"You know you don't mean that."

"Why not? What's the point if none of it is real?"

"It is for them," Zoe says. "It will take time."

"That's a bit of a cliché, isn't it?" I complain.

"It's relevant, though," she argues and I have to admit she is probably right. "Let's go to the forest. If two school girls walk into the garage midday, they will be asking questions. We can't exactly explain that we've bunked out of school when we're not allowed past the gates."

"Fair point," I sigh. "Fine; we can go to the forest. But, how are we getting there? It's way too far to walk and get back in time for our next class."

"Doesn't your cousin drive?"

"Not well."

"But he does? So, there we go; ask him," she says, ignoring my obvious dislike of the idea.

At seventeen, Brodie has only been driving for a few months. Debbie and Steve bought him his own car as soon as he was old enough and made sure he had the best instructor available. Yet somehow I still feel like I'm on a one way road to death whenever I'm in the car with him behind the driver's seat. So, the idea of having to do that again sounds like absolute hell to me.

But then again, it would make going to the forest so much quicker... Can he be trusted? I guess he was the one who gave me the diary in the first place; that's got to count for something.

"Do I have to?" I groan. Looking in her eyes, though, I know that it's futile to ask. "Alright, alright... I'm going!" I throw my hands up as I head from the bed. "Wait here until I'm back and be quiet. If anyone finds out that I sneaked you in here, I'm deader than dead."

She zips her lips shut with her fingers and I smile, shaking my head at the childishness. And I leave her there, closing the door softly behind me and knocking on Brodie's door down the hall. I barely have to wait a few seconds before he opens it, his gaming headphones already leaving a fluffy mark across his head.

"What's up?" he says. One hand is still on the door, ready to close it again; I guess I'll have to be quick in convincing him.

"I need you to drive us somewhere tomorrow."

"Us?" He raises an eyebrow, peering behind me like I've gone crazy.

"A friend," I add quickly. "Who isn't here."

"Sure she isn't," he replies. "Where do you need to go? Aren't you grounded?"

Gosh; why can no one just forget about it? It's like it's the most interesting thing going on at the moment and that people have nothing better to think about.

"Can you help me or not?" I ask bluntly, tired of playing games. I even fold my arms to show him just how much I cannot be bothered.

"If you give me some details," he says. "I'm not a mind reader."

"Ugh, fine," I groan, leaning in closer. "But you can't tell anyone. It's about my Mum's diary, the one you gave me."

"I didn't realise there was more than one," he jokes casually.

"Ha. Ha," I reply dryly. "Look, this is really important to me. Besides, you owe me."

"For what?" he says, surprised.

"I don't know - for being related to me," I suggest, taking a morsel of enjoyment in the face he pulls. "I read the first two entries. One was about Grayson's."

"The garage by the school?" he asks. I'm surprised he knows it even exists with how much time he spends at his computer. Even when he's walking back from sixth form, he has his headphones on, listening to a pod cast about his games usually.

"Yeah," I reply. "And the other place is the forest by the cliffs. That's where I need you to take Zoe and I tomorrow lunch."

"Year elevens aren't allowed out of school at dinner," he says, as though I don't already know that. "Oh, I'm with you. Hence why this is a secret."

"Exactly," I agree. "So, can you?"

"Hmmm, what's in it for me?" he asks, folding his arms just like I had before. It's in times like these that you can unfortunately tell we are related, as much as I hate to admit it.

"What do you want?" I roll my eyes. I expected nothing less from him, to be perfectly fair.

"There's a new game out next week but I'm twenty short," he states. "Help me out and I'll drive you there."

"Deal," I say quickly, knowing he might try and up his price. I hold my hand and he shakes it, solidifying my fate.

"Meet you in the car park after the bell," he says. "I'll hide you both in the back seat so the teacher on duty doesn't stop us. Now, are we finished?"

"Go back to your game," I say, waving him away. "But seriously, thank you. You're not as awful as you seem."

"Touché."

And the door closes.

It's the best outcome I could have gotten and I'm fully aware. Brodie might be the most annoying cousin ever - although, Dexter is pretty loud - but I know that we can't do this without him. Debbie and Steve never said how long my grounding will last but the thought of not being able to piece Mum's story together is upsetting to say the least. At least this way, we have a bit of freedom, even if it is at a cost.

And that's exactly what I say to Zoe when I head back to my room. She seems just as happy about it all as me, as though she really is a part of this now.

"You never even met her," I say. "Why do you want to do this?"

"For you," she replies simply. "You shouldn't have to go through this alone, even if you think you can. And yes, I know that I sound hella cliché but it's true. Besides, you like hanging out with me, I can tell."

"Hmmm," I say, realising a little too late that Brodie and I really are alike. "Just don't expect me to be your best friend or something. I don't do those. Anyways, what are we supposed to be looking for tomorrow? It's just a bunch of trees."

"How many times do I have to say it?" she laughs. "We're doing this to help you feel close to your Mum. We will tackle Grayson's another time and keep reading the diary but for now, you're going to be literally walking in her footsteps. Isn't that exciting?"

And nerve-wracking. So much so that I want to puke at the thought of it. I hate how it's all happened. She was a living, breathing person, going about her life like normal until she was hit by a car. Everything ended in that moment, even if she wasn't dead yet. Whoever was driving ruined my life and stole hers.

And I'll never forget that.

Twelve

When the bell for lunch arrives the next day, I'm practically running from the classroom. I clutch my bag tightly as I weave between other students in the crowded corridor, aiming only for the door to the car park. Once there, I step outside, grateful that it's quieter here, and clock Brodie's. He's already sat in the front; he must have come from a free period. I swear they will be the highlight of sixth form because lessons, at the moment, suck.

I bundle into the back, placing my bag at my feet.

"We just need to wait for Zoe," I say to him as I brush my hair away from my face. It's annoyingly windy outside so I'm not exactly looking forward to walking along the cliffs in it.

"Is that her?" he says. I look up and notice Zoe running clumsily across the car park towards us. She must have seen his car parked outside the house last night because she knows exactly which one we're in.

"Thanks for waiting," she says, bounding in next to me. "I couldn't have been further away!"

"It's okay," I say. "We've still got plenty of time. Are we ready to go now?"

"Yep," Brodie says. "There's a blanket on the backseat."

"I'm not cold," I reply, a little confused.

"To hide under, dumbass," he adds.

"Oh." I pick it up and bundle myself against Zoe on the floor, squished between the seats as close to the driver's side as possible; we'll be more hidden here. We're crouched as low as possible when we throw the blanket over our bodies and I don't think I've been this close to another person ever before. "Ready," I call to my cousin. And then I add to Zoe in a whisper: "sorry."

"It's okay," she says back, her voice just as low. "It's kind of funny. But I think I can smell Brodie's feet from here."

"Oh my God, Zoe," I cry. "Don't make me laugh now!"

"Guys!" Brodie complains; Zoe and I have a quiet chuckle before trying to be more serious. If we get caught, we'll have bigger problems than not being able to go to the forest and I'll be grounded for the rest of my life.

Underneath the covers, it's hard to know where we are. I can feel movement beneath us and the rev of Brodie's engine so we must have set off, but I wait patiently to hear the sound of the window being rolled down.

And it happens.

"Hi miss," he says.

"Going out today? That's rare," the teacher replies. I recognise the voice as belonging to Mrs Simmons, head of the sixth form at our school.

"There's a new game I want to go buy," he replies. That's a perfect Brodie kind of answer; no one would question whether or not it's true. "I'll be back for next period, though."

"Good," she says. "Well, I'll sign you out."

"Thanks, miss," he says and we're off again, driving away from the school. "You guys can come out now."

We clamber from under the blanket and climb back into the seats, buckling ourselves in before we reach the main roads; that's where Brodie's terrible driving will be noticeable and I'm not looking forward to it. But it's worth it.

"How are you feeling?" Zoe asks.

"Trying not to puke," I answer. "It's probably just Brodie, though."

"I can turn around, you know?" he says, catching my eyes in the mirror.

"Okay, okay," I say. "It's just weird. All of it. I feel like I don't even know her."

"It was just one lie," Zoe says, stroking my arm. I glare at her and she stops, realising how much I don't want to be touched. "And we still don't know why she didn't say anything."

"What lie?" Brodie asks. I could tell him to shove off and stop being so nosy but I guess he's a part of it now, in more ways than one.

"Mum didn't grow up in Green Haven," I explain. "Her diary entries are all about how she went to school here, *our* school. And all the places she is mentioning are from here."

"Weird," he says. But he doesn't press further.

"I don't understand why she'd erase it," I say. "I just want answers, for God's sake. I want to know what happened, why she was like she was. Who my Dad is."

"Woah, have I missed a chapter?" Brodie pipes up, swerving a little on the road as he tries to look at us.

"Oh my God," I practically scream. "Look at the frigging road!"

"Sorry, sorry," he says, steadying the car again. "But what are you on about?"

"She thinks the guy in the diary might be her Dad," Zoe explains for me, noticing that I'm struggling to answer.

"So, Eve never said anything about your Dad when she was alive?"

"Nothing," I say. "Absolutely nothing."

"Helpful," Brodie says. "Well, you still owe me twenty quid."

"You're paying him that much for a car ride?" Zoe asks me, shocked.

"And my silence," he adds. "That's the most important part. Anyways, I'm going to park here since I can't get any closer."

"Are you coming too?" I ask him, realising that he doesn't go to move once he parks.

"I'll wait here," he says. "Just be quick. We've got to be back for next period at school. I'm not having my lunch privileges taken away for this."

"As if you'd use them anyways," I say. "We won't be long, though." And I follow Zoe out of the car, slamming the door shut and beginning the small trek to the edge of the forest. It's colder than I'd like out here, the wind still raging around us, and I shiver to think about how close to the cliffs we are. But I know that we will have to go relatively close to them to get to the spot where everyone hangs out.

"Do you know where to go?" Zoe asks.

"Yeah," I say. "I've been there a few times myself. Like mother like daughter, I guess." Or, we're all just basic, doing the same thing that every other teenage in this God forsaken town does.

"Wish it wasn't so deep in," Zoe adds, looking a little spooked.

"It's the middle of the day," I explain, picking up my speed as I skip over branches. "We'll probably be able to see all the cars between the trees. And we've both got phones. Nothing to worry about."

Just memories. Memories of my dead Mum with a boyfriend from sixteen years ago.

Memories of a life that's gone forever.

"It's over there," I say. "In that clearing." I run through the trees to the spot I know it has to be. There are tree logs tipped over for seating, little marks etched into the wood from all the past lovers and friends who have been here before. And there, only a few meters away, is the edge of the cliff and a view of the sea. I could fall right now, tumbling over the side and crashing into the water below.

"Do you think she's written her name here too?" Zoe asks.

I whip my head away from the waves and look where she is, down at one of the logs, tracing her fingers over the letters.

"Probably," I say. "It would take forever to look, though."

"Don't you want to?" she asks. "It's kind of what we came here to do."

"Okay," I sigh. "We can try." And so I join her on the floor, reading countless names and rude phrases across the wood. After a few minutes, it feels futile, like we'll never find it, until...

"Gracie! Gracie, look!" Zoe squeals.

I practically fall over trying to scramble over. But there, on the underside of one of the logs is her name... and someone else's...

EVE + TOM

It has to be her… it just feels right. It's the first 'Eve' either of us have seen and so I choose to believe it; otherwise she just can't be here.

"There's only one way to find out," I whisper. As we look at one another, we're both thinking the same thing. "We have to go to Grayson's."

Thirteen

We stumble into the back of Brodie's car and I'm unsure how to feel. Physically, I'm smiling with relief. But inside, I'm burning with fear and worry and anxiety that it's not her. That Tom isn't the boy in the diary. That this is all just a wild goose chase by a miserable teenager who's been left behind.

"Any luck?" Brodie says.

"Maybe!" Zoe says excitedly. "We best get back, though. I don't know how long we were but it felt like ages."

"Yeah, you were cutting it close," Brodie replies. "I was about to ring you."

"Sorry we wasted your lunch hour," Zoe says.

It's awkward; I should be the one apologising since this is my thing but the words get stuck at the back of my throat. All I can think about is the tree… the names. It's all coming together; maybe I really will get answers.

It just feels weird that life has to go back to normal now. I've still got a few hours of school left and then I have to return to being grounded back at home. But I feel ready to read the next diary entry and I even think I want Zoe to be there again. It's not good; I don't want to become dependent on her and then lose her too. Loving people hurts and I don't think I can ever do it again.

The thought of it makes me nauseous.

"Right, fasten your seat belts," Brodie says, turning on the engine. I do as he says, barely taking my movements in. It's the same way I felt after it happened - numb, auto mode.

I stay like that all the way back, only breaking out of it to climb back into our hiding position under the blanket. This time, there's no childish giggling between us; there is only a hint of a smile in both of our eyes, one that means we're finally getting somewhere.

Once we're all parked up, I thank Brodie, passing him his money before he goes insane and begin my walk to my next class. It all feels perfectly mundane now and I'm itching to get home and read the next diary entry. Zoe says she will come home with me, even though it means climbing in through the window again. I'm actually starting to feel a bit bad about that now that we're kind of becoming friends. It's not like a set in stone kind of thing, though. It's a big fat maybe.

But meeting her after the last bell and seeing that smile on her face makes me question everything. She's always so genuinely excited to hang out and it makes me wonder about her other friends. Does she just not have any? Not that I can talk; I'm as billy no mates as they come but at least it's by choice.

"Ready?" she says, looking chirpy.

"Yeah," I say. "Can we walk past Grayson's?" I don't know why I say it; I don't even process it before it falls out of my mouth.

"Of course," she says and we start heading to Debbie's.

The garage is close by and as we go past it, I peer in through the glass at the office, hoping to catch a glimpse of someone. There's no one there but just as I'm about to lose hope, I see a man half underneath a car in the workshop part, only his legs visible. Could that be him? My Dad? I practically have to force my eyes away as we reach the end of the shop; I'd look weird just standing there goggling.

"You feeling okay?" Zoe asks me, looping her arm through mine in support. I take a deep breath and sigh, nodding my head in answer. "You did really well; that must have been hard."

"It just feels so much more real now," I let out. "Seeing the etching in the tree; it has to be hers. It *has* to."

"The diary will probably talk about it if is," she reminds me. "We will piece this all together. We'll find out who Eve really was."

And that's when I realise it fully; Zoe completely gets what all of this is about. I'm not just running after an old notebook because I'm sad; I'm doing it to keep her memory alive in the most authentic way possible. All I can hope is that this works, that the diary really does have all of the answers that I'm looking for.

When we get to my house, I'm almost scared to walk in without Zoe by my side. I'm becoming too attached, I think; I need to remember that people can't always stick around. But opening up the window to see her already halfway up the trellis, I'm grateful to have her around.

"I'm going to have to invest in a ladder," Zoe jokes as I haul her back through the window.

"At least I'm getting some exercise in," I chide back.

"Ouch," she laughs, swerving over the pane and landing comfortable on her feet. "Thank you, though. Now, onto the diary?"

"Yeah," I say. "We could go up in the attic; it might be more private there."

"That's fine by me," she agrees, slipping her shoes off. "We should hide them just in case someone comes in and thinks you've got someone over."

"I *do* have someone over," I joke. "But yeah, fair point. Just put them under the bed; they won't look there. Now, come on! I want to read Mum's diary!" I add this last bit with an embarrassing hint of desperation. It's becoming a lifeline of sorts, only not for the one I'm living now; my Mum isn't the only person I'm grieving.

Once we're up in the attic, we cosy ourselves on the sofa, curled up on either end with our feet up. For a moment, we look like two normal teenagers; just two girls hanging out after a long day at school. But

I'm not normal and I don't think I ever will be. How can I be with a past like mine?

"I wonder what the next one will be about," Zoe says as I begin to flick to our current page. "Maybe she will even say his name; if it's Tom, the etching has to belong to them."

"Fingers crossed," I say, before reading out the entry.

15th June 2001

Dear Diary,

I really thought I'd fumbled things with him. After our date, he didn't reach out, didn't wave back when I walked past Grayson's... he didn't even call our house phone. And so, I've spent the last week or so trying to accept that it's over before it's even really begun. Besides, there are so many other things that I should be focusing on; like the mock exams at the end of the year! I can't believe how soon they are! Before I know it, they will be here and I'll be sat in the sports hall, my pen scribbling away all of the things I've tried to remember. That's what should be important.

But, for some reason, I just can't get him out of my head. It's not like me. Boys are just a distraction from my real dreams; those that took me out of this town and into the life I really want. But he's here...

And I mean HERE. It's late now. My alarm clock read 02:23 before I sneaked away to the bathroom to write in my diary. So much has happened and I have to write quickly before he wakes up.

So, I came home from school like normal; having my dinner... doing my homework. I'd even done my half an hour of piano practice that Mum just had to sit and watch the whole time! I hate when she does that. I can't focus on playing the right keys.

Anyway! I was just about to read in bed when I heard a noise at my window. At first, it scared me; it was tinny but quiet, not loud enough to wake my parents or Debbie. But then I just became curious. I tiptoed over and pulled the curtain aside; there, hiding by the back of my parent's car, was Tom.

"Tom?" we both blurt out at the same time.

"It's him? The etching in the forest; that's really your Mum!" Zoe exclaims.

"Shhh," I say, remembering that the floor isn't sound proof. I'm still grounded, after all. "But it must be. Surely?"

"I'd say so," Zoe confirms, nodding along. "Keep going; I want to find out what happened."

I wasn't sure if it was even him to begin with, but after my eyes acclimated to the darkness, I spotted his buzz cut and knew it had to be him.

"What are you doing?" I said to him, as quietly as I could while still being heard. "Why are you here?"

"I wanted to see you," he replied. "Can I come in?"

I hesitated here, wondering what I should do, what it all meant. But could I say no? He'd never give me a third chance; he's too cool and I'm just... well, me.

So I told him to meet me at the front door and somehow, I managed to get him all the way to my room without anyone finding out. I'm quite surprised; I was half waiting for someone to notice and tell me off, kicking him out so I didn't have to.

That way he can at least put the blame elsewhere and I can take a little longer to ease into it all.

But as soon as we got to my room and the door was closed, he didn't give me chance to pause. He started kissing me... hard and passionate. Maybe he does like me? He's a seventeen year old boy, though. So, I guess I could have been anyone and he would have been happy. But it was my house he came to... It's my bed he's now sleeping in.

I have to go. I'm taking too long! I'll write more tomorrow.

Eve

"So," Zoe says.

I close the book, holding it close against my chest.

"I don't think we need to read the next one to know what happened," I whisper. My mind wanders to how she must have felt in that moment; terrified of letting him down but scared to do what it took. I'm a twenty-first century teenager; I know what it means, I know what it's leading to. And I hate it, how she felt like that.

I've been wanting to find out who my Dad is for years, a whole lifetime, but I don't want it to be *him*.

But I have to accept that the timeline makes sense; my Mum had me before she even finished school and here she is, her first year at sixth form, messing around with this Tom character.

"You feeling okay? That was a lot," Zoe asks.

"Yeah," I nod. "Yeah."

"It's okay if you're not," she adds.

"I said I'm fine," I spit. "Look, can we just finish up here for tonight? I've got homework to do."

"Sure," she says, though I think she knows I'm lying about why I want her gone. I don't care, though. I just need to be alone.

Fourteen

The night passes by quietly as I think everything over, cycling through all the new information I've learned about my Mum. With each diary entry, I feel one step further to uncovering the truth in her story but I also feel like I don't know her at all. She'd told me so many things about her childhood, yet she had never mentioned any of this. As far as I had known, she lived in Green Haven, had perfectly imposing parents and had me when she was young. That's it.

When Brodie gave me this diary, I thought I'd be reading incoherent ramblings from the teenage version of my Mum. Instead, Eve Myers is becoming more real to me than ever before, casting the truth she has been hiding into the light. And now there are two different Eve's in my head: the girl in the diary and the woman in my life.

It's all becoming too much… too heavy. I'm only sixteen.

…

"Gracie! Gracie!" a voice calls. I rush to sit up in my bed, thinking it was maybe from my nightmare. But no. The door opens wide and Debbie is stood there, buttoning up her work shirt. "You're going to be late."

"For what? It's Saturday," I complain, throwing my body back onto the mattress. I barely got any sleep last night; I just want to drift back away and spend the day rotting in bed, doing nothing other than feeling my Mum's absence.

"You said you'd go with Steve and the boys," she says, closing the door again.

Why on earth would I agree to go anywhere with those three?

And then it dawns on me.

I rush from the bed, practically throwing the duvet onto the floor. Before doing anything else, I check the time on my phone: 9:30... I've only got half an hour to be ready and at the door. Luckily, I'm not the kind of person who needs a long time; I fluff up the waves in my hair, smudge eyeliner across the crease and stumble into an outfit. I look presentable enough, encased in dark purples and black the way I always used to dress.

People always used to wonder if I really was Eve's daughter. She was so bright and colourful, quite fitting for a florist, yet I was, stereotypically, the complete opposite. Mum never cared, though.

"As long as you're happy," she'd say.

But that all changed when I moved to my grandma's house. Jean Myers was as strict as she always had been, complaining about everything I did or didn't do. They were the worst months and that's not just because they were the first few after Mum died. That woman made my life more hellish than it should have been and I was almost grateful when she could no longer care for me.

Until I realised how much worse it was living with Debbie and Steve and their two stinky sons that is.

What all three of them have in common, though, was that Gracie was erased. I was simply the burden placed on them, another to mouth to feed and another teenager to keep out of trouble. Anything that possibly made me look like a problem was wiped away. Or, at least, they *tried* to get rid of it.

One of the early signs of this was whenever Debbie would rip down my band posters.

"It doesn't look tidy!" she'd said as she'd stood on my bed, pulling them down. "You're a young lady; you need to start acting like it."

But no matter how many times she prised the posters from the wall, I put them back up. It took three months for her to give up but she barely steps into my room anymore. How is she that offended by pictures of bands?

Over time, she'd learned to step back and let me be Gracie. Well, to some extent. She's not exactly over the moon about some of the things that I like but I'm past caring.

Anyway, I'm getting off track, thinking too much about things that aren't important.

I grab a bag and slide Mum's diary into it, as well as my purse, and tie up the laces to my Docs. Looking in the mirror, I sigh, wishing I could know what Mum would think of me now. I doubt she'd be proud; I haven't exactly done anything worthy of that since she left.

"You coming?" Brodie's voice is muffled through the door.

"Yep," I say back, swinging around and joining him.

...

With everything else that's been going on, I'd forgotten about our plans for this day. But now all of the excitement creeps into my stomach and as I'm bounding into the back of the car, I don't even care that Dexter is playing his DS beside me on full volume. Usually, it would annoy me but as soon as we get there, I can go my own way.

"I'm surprised Mum's still letting you come," Brodie says from the passenger seat. "I thought you'd be grounded forever."

"I still am," I groan. "But she probably didn't want me in the house alone." I know it's the only reason I'm still being allowed to go; she's terrified of what I'll get up to with no adult in the house. Fair play, to be honest; I've got a whole bucket list of things I want to do.

"Ready, kids?" Steve says, turning on the car.

"Uh huh," I reply.

"Right, then," he says. "Belts on; York, here we come."

…

As the nearest city, York was always the place that Mum and I would go to when we wanted a day out to go shopping or sit in cafes. It's a place where only she has ever taken me, until now. But there was no way I was letting a city day slip from under me; I love them too much. I can already smell the food stands along the market street… the waft of burgers cooking and hot chocolate filling the air.

It's best at Christmas time when all the fairy lights are strung above the stalls and there are festive songs playing. Every year without fail, she'd take me. She knew how much I revelled in it all; while she was perfectly happy in tiny, little Green Haven, I wanted much more. I was never made to be a small town kind of girl; I thrive in the city and she could see it… she made sure I had plenty of days here, even if she maybe couldn't afford it as much as she made out.

So now, as we begin the task of finding a space in the parking garage, the excitement creeps up inside of me. As soon Steve turns the key, I'm out the door.

"See you later!" I call.

"Be back here for quarter to five," Steve calls after me.

"Yeah, yeah," I say but I'm barely listening. I've got pretty much the rest of the day to myself, to be Gracie, to be the girl who always came here with her Mum. Almost like she's still alive.

Fifteen

My first stop is to get as far away from my Uncle as cousins as possible so that I don't have to worry about bumping into them for a while. This takes me on a long walk through the centre of town. I'm itching to go into all the shops I pass but I know that I can go through them later on. For now, they're too close to Steve and the boys and the whole point of today is that I can be by myself for a bit.

Once I'm far enough away, I finally allow myself to begin the trip properly. The first part? A coffee shop my Mum and I would always sit in.

I'm standing outside of it now, looking up at it. From all my memories here, it's never really changed much, only little bits here and there to keep up to date. But other than that, I could go back ten years and easily recognise it. I'm grateful for that; for a moment, I can pretend it's the time before all of this happened.

As I said, it's only for a moment because I don't plan on forgetting any of the last year once I'm inside.

"Two lattes, please," I say, stepping up to the counter.

"Any syrups?" the girl asks.

"Just gingerbread, please," I reply, dropping the coins into her palm. It takes only a minute before she's handing the glasses to me and I take it to the table by the window, falling back into the sofa. I place the two cups in front of me, laying one out a little further from me. This was *our* seat so I'm lucky no one else had taken it.

And then I slide out Mum's diary, curling up and tucking it against my legs. I might not have Zoe here to hold my hand through this but I don't need it. For a whole year, I held my own damn hand and I got good at it; I can still do this by myself. Besides, it feels fitting, reading her own words opposite the chair she would talk to me from. It's like she's here… sat with me, drinking her own coffee, even if there is only an empty chair in front of mine.

17th June 2001

Dear Diary,

I'm sorry I didn't write yesterday like I said I would. I was so busy and just didn't get the chance but I'm here now!

Okay, let me continue with what happened the other night with Tom. So, he was kissing me, holding my face with his rough fingers. It felt so strange. It was my first kiss, after all. But I never thought it would be like that; so full on. I don't know if that's quite the right way to describe it but it's close enough.

And then he started guiding me towards my bed. I'm surprised he even knew where it was in the room; he'd barely looked at anything before his lips were on mine. But he did it all the same and I'd fallen back onto the duvet. I wasn't sure what I was supposed to be doing so I just kind of let him take the lead. All I kept thinking was that a boy actually wanted to kiss me! Me! Eve Myers!

Debbie's a few years older than me; she's actually quite old, really, because she's in her twenties already. I'm not ready to be twenty three; I still feel younger than seventeen! But she didn't have her first kiss until she was eighteen and it was with Steve. And now they're married!

I can't help but wonder if that means Tom and I will go down that same path… I guess there's no telling and I don't even know what I want to happen.

Anyways, I'm going off track!

At this point, I could tell he wanted to do something more. He'd started to touch me, sending his hands all over my body... under my top... across my tummy. My stomach was practically doing somersaults over it and it even had me feeling a little sick. But that's probably just normal; Tom obviously knows what to do in these situations so I trust him.

But I got scared AGAIN!

"What's up?" he had said.

I'd clenched my legs together for like the fourth time by that point and it was always when his hand had inched closer.

"Don't you like it?"

"I do," I'd replied. "I do."

But did I? I don't think 'like' was the right word. I wasn't exactly enjoying it as much as I thought I should be but what did I know? This was SUPPOSED to feel good so I must have been doing something wrong.

"I'm not going to do it if you're going to ruin the moment," is what he'd said. But all I could say was:

"This is a moment? We're having a moment?"

I must have sounded so innocent!

"Well, yeah," he had replied. "What else would it be?"

"I don't know." Because I didn't know any of this.

"So, can I actually do it, then?"

I wanted to say 'yes' but I just couldn't say it for some reason. Instead, I said nothing, did nothing... and he must have thought I meant it was okay to carry on. And maybe it was!

I don't knowwwwww.

But he did it all the same and I guess it wasn't too bad. I've just always had all these notions about my 'first time'. Who it would be with... where it would be... how it would happen! And it certainly wasn't as interesting as I always predicted but this is real life, after all. Tom's probably slept with loads of girls; if he wanted it to happen like this, then this must be how people do it.

So... I did it!

I had sex for the first time and I can't tell a single person. It's probably for the best; Mum would kill me.

Anyways, there's the update! I'll write again soon! <3

Eve

Reading how confused she was hurts me so much that I almost wish I could go to Grayson's right now and give this Tom guy a black eye. Every time I read another entry about him, he annoys me even more. Mum must have been so insecure and naive when she was younger to not realise how bad he was. He doesn't even sound like he cares about her... but she thinks she *needs* him.

If this Tom really is my Dad, I don't think I want anything to do with him. No wonder Mum started lying about everything; I wouldn't want to relive any of this either.

I put the diary down on the table, needing a mental break, and have a sip of my coffee. The one I bought for Mum sits there; I don't even know why I got it. Maybe it was muscle memory? Maybe it was an attempt to try and hold onto something I've lost? I don't know; but it's painful.

"Are you meeting someone?" The girl from the counter comes over, pointing at the cup I've been staring at like a loony.

"Uhm, no," I admit.

"Right..." comes the confused reply. "Can I get you anything else?"

I look towards Mum's seat. She'd always reply here, asking for some sort of Bakery item for us both to share. But she can't do that now.

"I kind of recognise you," she says. "Have you been here before?"

"Yeah," I reply. "A few times each year."

"With your Mum, right?"

A pang.

"Uh huh."

"Where is she? Is that who the coffee is for?" she asks, prying a bit too much.

"It's not really your business, is it?" I don't care if it's rude. She doesn't have to be putting her nose in, trying to find out all the details like I'm some runaway or something.

"Well, I was just checking you were okay," she says, still as kindly as before. She turns on her heel softly and heads back over to the counter, watching me over her shoulder with worry.

I suppose I do look a bit strange, having coffee with no one, just an empty seat and a mass of memories. But what else am I supposed to do? This is important: I need to remember Eve Myers properly and that means doing the hard things. Like reading about idiotic boys from nearly two decades ago... and sitting in coffee shops we used to go to together... and visiting places that used to mean something to her.

"Excuse me," a voice calls. It can't be the woman from before; this person is a man.

I look up, drowning under his height. He's older than I predicted, with small wrinkles forming around his eyes and his brown hair beginning to grey. But his eyes... they're piercing; brown and bold.

"Uhm, yes?" I ask back, curious why he's bothering me.

"I don't suppose you're meeting anyone?" he replies. He glances at the empty chair in front of me just as I do. Of course I'm not actually waiting for anyone but why would I tell him that? He's creeping me out.

"Yes," I add bluntly.

"Oh," he says, his eyes fluttering a little. "Right."

The longer I leave it to reply, the more his body language begins to shift. He's gone from confident to worried, unsure of how to hold himself.

"Are you alright?" I ask. I'm not really that worried about him but it's the polite thing to do, even if he is freaking me out.

"Yeah, yeah," he adds, waving his arm at me as though shooing me off. And then he's leaving the cafe, turning right once he's out of the door.

That was odd. *Really* odd. Part of me is even hoping that Steve is nearby just in case because I don't really feel safe anymore. I'm only sixteen and I'm pretty much alone here. If anything were to happen, would my Uncle get here in time? I shiver to think about what could have happened as I finish off the last of my coffee. I don't want to be hanging around here if that guy comes back. Besides, I've got places to be.

Sixteen

It feels a bit of a waste to leave Mum's coffee sat there on the table but I can't drink it myself; that would somehow be even worse. No, I'll leave it there and then I can pretend that she's staying behind to finish it off while I head to the next place. Yes. That's what's happening.

But just as I step outside of the cafe, my phone dings.

> Hey!
> I hope ur feeling okay today.

> Mum needs to get her car looked at so I suggested we go to Grayson's!

> I'll keep u updated. I hope it's okay that I'm going.

I think about it for a moment. It would probably be fair of me to be mad about her going there without me but it's not like I've had a chance. She can do some digging and let me know what's going on. At least this way, there's less chance of me getting hurt. I don't think that I could handle seeing Tom right now.

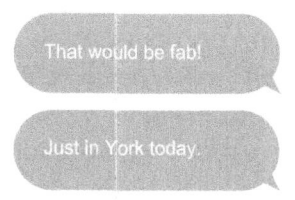

> That would be fab!

> Just in York today.

She replies quicker than I expect her to; she was probably hunched over her phone, waiting for me to tell her that I don't hate her for it.

> Brill! Heading there soon but I hope u have a fab day!

> Thanks, u too!

She hearts my message, the conversation clearly finished, and I put my phone back in my coat pocket. It's cold out here; most likely I'm feeling it more now because I've been tucked away with a warm coffee. Pulling the fabric around my neck, I walk down the street to where I know the donut stall will be.

My Mum loved donuts and I really cannot describe how much. It was a staple part of every grocery shop, an important bit she always saved for last so it wouldn't be squished at the bottom of the trolley. Sometimes they would be chocolate but her favourite was the sugar ring ones. She said that people always underestimated them, even though they had the best taste. Looking back now, she probably liked them because they reminded her of a secret seaside town she grew up in and lied about...

I push the thought out of my mind; that's not important. What matters is why she felt like she had to keep it from me.

The donut stall doesn't have a line; it's practically inviting me to come and place my order. So I do.

"Could I get five please?" I ask the woman. Mum and I always used to get this deal because they do five for four and then we'd split the extra one between us. I don't know what I'll do with her share today; I guess it might end up being another coffee situation.

"That's three quid, lovely," she says. I hand over the cash and stand about waiting, shuffling my shoes against the ground. Peering up only once tells me that she's making them new, letting them roll through the machine so that they will be all hot and fresh. I can't help but smile; they taste way better this way.

"Here you are," she passes me the bag of donuts once they're done; they're warm against my fingers.

"Thank you," I say and I head on over to a bench opposite the stall to eat them. I'm in no rush to cover all of the shops here like I used to do; this day is about something different. I can take my time and bask in the moments I'm trying to create. Such as reading the next entry because today feels like the perfect time to connect with her and piece together the dots.

30th June 2001

Dear Diary,

Ever since Tom and I did it, he's barely spoken to me. The day after it happened, I stopped by the garage. I thought he'd want to see me, to talk about it... maybe to even ask me to be his girlfriend. But he kept brushing me off and saying that I was going to get him into trouble with his Dad if I kept hanging around. So I left but I kept replaying it over and over in my head.

I don't know what I did wrong. Maybe I was really bad at sex... I haven't done it before so it's *not like I've had chance to practice. Tom's probably not used to that; he knew exactly what he was doing, all the right places to touch me, to kiss me...*

Aghhhh. I'm thinking about it all over again now. I don't even know if I liked it or not so why can't I get it out of my mind?

Anyway, I do wish he would just talk to me. It feels really mean, maybe like he's led me on. I really want to speak to Debbie about it because she's been with Steve for ages. She knows about these kinds of things. But I think she would tell our parents and I can't risk that. So I'm just going to have to figure it out for myself.

Eve

Once again, I'm realising that this Tom guy is such a dickhead. Horny. But still a dick.

I put the notebook down beside me on the bench and start eating one of the donuts. Within seconds, there's a sprinkle of sugar on my lap, coating my jeans in a silver glitter. Debbie would tell me to eat more tidily but Mum would just laugh at how annoying they are to eat and pretend to wear a lipstick out of the sugar. I can feel dots of it against my lip now but she's not there to enjoy the moment with me.

Luckily, I don't have long to dwell on it.

> Heading there now

> How's York!

Coldddddd

> Well, it is winter haha.

> Did u read anymore?

We both know what she means. It's not some fictional book she's asking about; it's the diary, the only thing that I can seem to focus on these days.

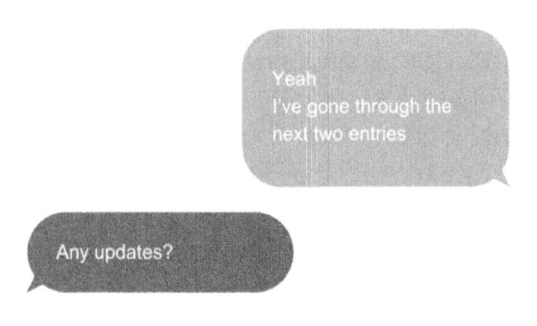

Yeah
I've gone through the next two entries

> Any updates?

> Just about how much of a nob Tom was. Ignored her after, u know?

> Just slept with her and then wanted nothing to do with her.

> That's awful! I can't imagine how difficult that was for Eve.

> Neither. I hate him.

> He may have changed…

> Doubt.
> Anyways, let me know how the garage goes.

> Will do!

Part of me is incredibly nervous to hear what she says. He might not even work there anymore... even if it's still owned by his family, he could have gone on to work elsewhere. Though, he dropped out of sixth form. Who knows what his plan was?

But I can't stay here on this bench forever... I eat the rest of my half of the donuts, putting the other two and half into my bag. I'll figure out what to do with them later. For now, there's a record store calling my name.

Seventeen

Mum and I always shared a love for music. The house was alive with it whenever either of us was at home, mainly because she spent pretty much a week's worth of food on a record player once. From then on, we got the most use out of it, thrifting anything we could find and would enjoy to play on it.

To be honest, I think she loved the idea of it because of that one show, *Gilmore Girls*. We would watch it together all the time, shouting and throwing popcorn at the screen whenever Dean walked into the shot. We both hated his character with a passion but I'm starting to wonder if there was more to it. Maybe she linked Dean with Tom, comparing their actions? But they seem awful in completely opposite ways: while one was perhaps a little too loved up, the other didn't have enough of it. Either way, it both boils down to the fact that I don't like either of them.

Anyway, so here I am at the record store in York; the one that we would always rifle through in case we found anything worth adding to our growing collection. I still have them all in my room; I literally refused to part with them, saying that they were just as much mine as they were hers. Anything else she left behind was either sold or donated, funding the pockets of my Aunt and Uncle for having to take me in. They could have just done it from the goodness of their hearts, though. Bit rude, really.

Once I'm inside, I'm centred in a labyrinth of storage units for the hundreds, if not thousands, of records that they store. I barely know where to look; I'm overwhelmed by the choice and smiling awkwardly at the old man perched behind the till.

"Welcome," he says. I nod back to him, scuttling to the back of the store and flipping through a random section. I don't even know who these artists are but they have cool enough covers, at least. I'm not sure if I'll buy anything yet, though. If I think there's one that Mum would have insisted we get, then I'll cave. But I'm not buying one for the sake of it.

"That's a good one," a familiar voice says. But I don't need to take any guesses.

It's the man from before.

"What do you want?" I ask; I'm not dancing around the point this time. He's followed me here and that's weird. "You can't hurt me here. There's someone right over there." I point at the man at the counter; he's so old that he probably wouldn't be much help to me if anything does happen but he could at least call the police.

"I'm not going to hurt you," he whispers.

"Who are you?" I ask him, staring him dead in the eyes. I watched a documentary once about how if you're face to face with a shark, you shouldn't turn your back on them: you need to deal with them straight on. Now, this man isn't a shark but I don't fancy cowering under him.

"You know," he says.

"No, I don't," I reiterate. "Otherwise I wouldn't be asking you."

"She deserved it, you know?" is all he says.

What does that even me? She? My Mum, maybe? Perhaps he's just drunk... but he doesn't look it. No, those eyes aren't wasted; they're sinister.

"Who? Deserved what?" I ask.

But he just smiles.

What the fuck?

And then he's gone, walking from the shop in a much more confident manner than he'd had at the cafe. It's getting really strange now, though. Once was fair enough; he could have been any random weirdo. But twice? Following me and talking in riddles? Nah. I'm not doing this.

I pull up Zoe and mine's messages, giving her the unexpected update.

> There's this really creepy guy following me around. What do I do??

She replies instantly, the three little dots appearing only a moment later.

> Are u okay?

> Has he done anything??

> He said that "she deserved it"... don't know what he's on about tho.

> u don't suppose he's talking about, well, u know who?

> Maybe.

> I've got an update too

> Oh yeah?

Nothing, and I mean *nothing*, could have prepared me for what she was about to say.

> Tom isn't here.

> He's in York for the day.

> Wait. What.

> I think I know who that guy is. And if it is him, I don't think ur safe.

> He wouldn't tell me who he is... but he obviously knows who I am.

> Oh my god, Zoe. What if he is Tom? What if he's my dad????

But she doesn't open this last message; there's no 'read' receipt underneath my concerns. She must be busy over there; I guess I'll have to try and be patient. All I do know is that I don't want to be by myself here any longer. I swipe away from Zoe's chat and open up Steve's, ringing his number without hesitation. It rings a few times but he eventually picks up.

"Gracie? You good?" he asks, his voice a little crackly.

"Can you meet me? I'm a little worried," I say, hating how I'm going to have to admit that I'm scared.

"Why? Has something happened?" I'm surprised to hear the concern in his voice; I honestly thought he'd just tell me to grow up which, I guess he can still do once I tell him what's going on.

"Someone is following me; there's this man," I tell him. The words wobble out and I hate how weak I sound. I look completely bad ass in my Docs and eyeliner; but I feel vulnerable.

"Okay, where are you?" he asks.

"The record shop by the church," I tell him. "Please can you come straight away? I'm going to stay in here."

"Yes, definitely," he says. "Dext, Brodie! Come back over here; we've gotta go." And the call dies.

I guess all I can do now is wait awkwardly, rifling through the records aimlessly. I don't expect to find anything good, especially since the boys will be here any minute, but when I come across a rare copy of my Mum' favourite album, it feels too good to be true. But there it is... a 1987 edition with some of Cher's songs.

She'd always preferred to listen to older music, hence why she was a fan of vinyls in the first place. She said they were classy and should never be forgotten about just because they were old.

She never even got a chance to *be* old. Someone took that opportunity from her in a moment and now I'm living in the aftermath of a single mistake. And was it even an accident? I can't help but wonder... I don't want to believe that a good and honest person could do something like that and then just drive away like it was nothing. But, if someone did it on purpose, I can't put it past them not to care about the bigger picture. I may only be sixteen but I'm not completely naive. I know that there are horrible people out there, people who are capable of something like this.

But the chances of finding this particular vinyl, especially when I wasn't even trying, feels unlikely. Yet, it's happening. I'm holding it in my hands and she would have loved it.

"Excuse me," I say to the man at the desk. "Please could I get this?"

"It's thirty quid," he says, looking at me with an eyebrow raised as though he thinks I can't afford it. To give him credit, I am a sixteen year old; I don't exactly look like I've got a wad of cash in my pocket. But I bring out three ten pound notes all the same, handing them over. "Would you like a bag?"

"Yes, please," I say.

A moment later, he passes me my purchase and it's perfect timing too.

"Gracie?" Steve says, hurrying into the store with the boys. Poor Dexter is red in the face, almost as though he's been running. "Are you alright?"

"Yeah, I'm fine," I say, pulling a face. Why is he *that* concerned? Like, calm down. I'm not dead. But he doesn't look satisfied with my answer.

"You're gonna have to stay with us for the rest of the day," he says. "It's not safe to be out by yourself." Something tells me that this is about more than just an independent situation… there's something he's not telling me. "Come on." And now he's holding his arm out as though he's going to walk around with his hand over my back.

"You're being weird," I say.

"You've just said you're being followed by a man," he said. "I'm not going to leave you by yourself and if you see him again, let me know. If we need to, we can call the police."

"The police?" That makes it sound so real, so dangerous.

"Well, yes," he says. "Now, if you want to stay in York, you have to stay with me."

"Fine," I sigh. I did call for his help, after all; I can't have an attitude about it now.

"Tough luck," Brodie smiles at me.

…

I spend the afternoon being dragged around boring stores. They mainly go into trainer shops, trying on multiple pairs that they're literally never going to buy. At one point, I even have to stand awkwardly on the sidelines as Brodie buys some more underwear.

But I can't really complain. Not even when Dexter insists he needs to pee and we have to flurry to find some toilets.

Wanna know why?

Because that creepy guy is there again, standing across the road as we wait for my cousin to relieve his bloody bladder. But Steve's in the cubicle with him, deep inside the building, and Brodie and I are exposed on the street.

"Brodie," I say, scared to look away from the man. "Brodie!"

"Oh my God, what?" he sighs.

"He's there," I tell him. "Look. What do we do?"

I sense Brodie moving beside me, his head pointing in the same direction as mine. But the man doesn't waver.

"Who the fuck is he?" he says to me.

"I have an idea but I don't know for certain," I admit. He whips his face in my direction and I can't help but look at him. "I think it might be one of my Mum's old boyfriends."

"Why would you think that?" he asks.

"The guy in the diary... Tom," I begin, my voice shaking. All I can hope is that he stays well away, watching from a distance. "And Zoe... she went to Grayson's earlier; apparently Tom isn't there because he's in York today. Where we are... and this guy, the one over there... he said that she deserved it."

"Who deserved what?" Brodie questions.

"I think he means my Mum." My voice is barely holding it together, each word more difficult to stumble through. "I think Tom killed my Mum."

PART TWO

Eighteen

"Why would Tom kill your Mum, though?" Brodie asks, shaking his head. "They haven't seen each other since they were teenagers. Surely anything they could have argued about back then would be water under the bridge after all this time?"

"Unless that something was a living and breathing thing," I say slowly. It's all coming together; the more I see this man, the more certain I am that he's Tom, that he's my Dad. We kind of look the same, especially our hair. But I also look like my Mum so it's not like it's confirmation or anything; my wavy dark locks could just be what she has passed down to me. But I feel it in my gut; that has to count for something.

"Wait, what are you saying?" Brodie stumbles.

"That Tom might be Daddy dearest? Yeah," I say. "But I don't get why he's randomly started showing up now after all these years."

"Well, he might have showed up a year ago," Brodie reminds me. "And who knows what was happening before that. How far through the diary are you?"

"Only June 2001," I say, remembering how many years that thing spans. "Brodie, don't tell anyone this but I'm actually a bit scared. He's probably psychotic, especially if he's the driver that hit her."

"What I want to know is how he's got away with it all this time," Brodie answers.

I'm not going to lie, I'm kind of surprised how supportive he's being. He even put his phone away at some point in the conversation, all of his attention now on my current problem.

"They never even found the car, even with all the technology we've got nowadays. There's something off about it all. Something weird."

"You're telling me," I say, staring at the man coldly.

"Ready?" Steve says, coming out of the bathrooms with Dexter's hand in his. "Why are you looking like that? We didn't take that long."

"The man that followed her is back at it," Brodie says, not even giving me a chance to explain. Steve's face turns into fear as he looks all around us, until finally his eyes land on the stranger across the road.

"It can't be," he whispers.

"What? What is it?" I stumble. There is definitely something he is hiding from me, I know it for certain now. But why can't they tell me? It's clearly got something to do with me, otherwise I wouldn't be the one being followed.

"We need to get to the car," is all he says. He grabs my hand; Dexter and I are like puppets as he pulls us along. "Brodie, stand on the other side of her."

Brodie does as he's told, even though neither of us knows what's going on.

"Don't let him near her," he says again.

"Steve, seriously," I say, trailing along beside him. "What's going on?"

"We should have left straight away!" he says but he's just twittering to himself now as though we're not even here.

I peer over my shoulder quickly, looking at the man. As I predicted, his gaze follows the path we are taking and then, after looking from side to side, he begins to walk after us.

"Steve, he's following us!" I say. I'm too scared now to act cool like I always try to appear; this man is truly terrifying and my heart is pounding a thousand miles a minute. It feels the same as when I was running through the hospital corridors looking for my Mum's room after the accident, worried that I was going to lose her. And I did... I *did* lose her. And this man might be responsible, hiding from the police in plain sight.

"Walk faster," my Uncle orders.

"Daddy, I don't like it," Dexter wails.

And hearing his tiny little child voice doesn't grate me for the first time ever; the little wobble in his words just sends an unwanted thrill through my body as I realise how serious this all is.

Mum's death was labelled as an accident, a hit and run by a scared driver who was terrified to own up and be punished for something that they didn't mean to do. But I never wanted to believe that it was purposeful, that someone could put their foot on the pedal and speed into her, knocking her to the ground and leaving her all alone in the dark on the side of the road. That's just messed up.

I'm more than relieved when we make it back to the parking garage, running up the stairs to get to level three where we'd left the car. There's no knowing if he's still following after us, only a few flights of stairs below us, but the sound of doors swinging open below us tells me that it's a possibility.

By the time I reach the last step, I'm literally tripping over it to get out of the stairwell.

"Into the car," Steve orders, unlocking it as we all bound towards it.

Dexter and I fly into the back and I help him buckle his car seat and my own seat belt as Brodie and Steve take the front seats. And then I hear the doors lock, that little blot of noise protecting us from anything outside of the vehicle. But if he really did kill my Mum, then he's no stranger to doing things that he definitely shouldn't be doing to get what he wants.

"Who is he?" I ask again. I need to know if it's really him... if it's Tom, if it's my Dad... how the fuck Steve recognises him.

"Not now, Gracie!" he shouts back, reversing out of the parking space. Just as we begin to drive through the maze to get downstairs, I see the man opening the stairwell door... looking directly at us with anger. He knows that this is our car.

He knows that this is our car.

This has been going on much longer than today.

"I know there's a speed limit," Brodie says. "But he's literally meters away from us right now."

Steve glares at him, looking as though the idea is ridiculous. But I change my mind when he takes the corner to get to the slope, throwing all of us to the side abruptly.

"Sorry," he says as he heads down the ramp.

I look behind us, staring out of the back window.

"He's not moving," I say. "He's just standing there. Wait, no, he's calling someone!"

"Good," Steve says, continuing through the circuit to get out of this damn parking garage.

"Not good!" I complain. "That means he's not alone in whatever the fuck this is."

"We'll sort it later," is all Steve says. "Just let us get home first."

But I don't want to sort it later. I want people to start telling me what is going on; I need the answers. And maybe I have something that can get me a few... I open my bag, sliding out Mum's diary and turning frantically to the next entry. If Steve won't tell me anything, maybe seventeen year old Eve Myers can.

27th August 2001

Dear Diary,

    I haven't written in forever, I know. There's just been so much on, so much to worry about. There were the exams (which I think went fine) and then Debbie decided she was going to move closer to home again so we had to help her sell her house. For a while, I was distracted. Tom had become just a boy that I'd had sex with once but wouldn't again and I was starting to accept that.

    But I can't ignore it anymore.

    I missed my period. And then I missed another. So I took a test.

    I'm pregnant... and Tom's the Dad. I don't know what to do, though! Whenever I try to talk to him, he just brushes me away or ignores me. I keep hoping that if he maybe knew what it was that I need to tell him, he might listen. But he's already started seeing someone new... he doesn't want anything to do with me, let alone a baby.

    I could get an abortion. I know that I could. But I just don't know if I can mentally do that. I *have nothing to give a child, yet. I'm only a child myself! But when I think about all the judgmental looks I'd get if I keep it, it terrifies me.*

The hard part will be telling my parents. I won't be able to get an abortion without them knowing. Everyone talks here… it would spread quickly and I'd never live it down. I don't want my baby to be born into shame.

So, I need to tell them and I need to do it soon so I have time to decide what I want to do.

Anyways, that's the update. I'm scared of everything that could or might happen right now… but I need to make the right decision about it all. I might be seventeen but I know that this is important.

Eve

Well, I needed confirmation and I guess that is it. Tom is my Dad. Tom Grayson is my Dad. Gosh, that sounds weird to say. I didn't really think I'd ever know but here I am with all the evidence I'd need to prove it. And if the man who followed me really is him, then what on earth did my Mum do to piss him off?

Nineteen

I get too travel sick to read anymore of her diary in the car but luckily we get home soon enough. Steve even parks in the garage (you have no idea how rare this is) so that we don't have to be outside to get into the house.

"Why are you back so early?" Debbie says, watching us all piling into the kitchen.

"Why aren't you at work?" Steve says. "You said you have meetings all day."

"They were cancelled," she says. And that's when I notice there's a glass of wine and chocolates sat on the island counter in front of her.

"We can discuss that later," Steve replies, trying his best to ignore it, though I can see he is practically bursting to know what's going on with his wife. "We need to talk about you know what."

"You know what?" I question. "You guys can't keep pretending like you don't know anything; I'm right here and I'm involved now. Though, by the looks of things, I've probably been involved this whole time without even knowing it."

Steve and Debbie exchange a worried glance with each other. I could literally punch them right now. Somehow, Mum's memorial service feels like nothing compared to all of this. Wearing black to a funeral-related event seems less important than realising that the only reason we were at a funeral event was because she was murdered.

"You have to tell me," I say. "Please."

"Right," Debbie sighs. "Dexter, Brodie, go upstairs."

"Woah, I gotta know too," Brodie says.

"Brodie has been helping me," I admit. But then I realise that my Aunt and Uncle can't know that I have the diary. "He's just been surprisingly supportive."

"That's unlike him," Debbie says. If we were in any other situation, I'd take this as an opportunity to laugh at how savage that was. But my funny bone is switched off now. "Okay, you can stay. Dexter, go play in your room for a bit, alright?"

"I don't want to be by myself," he whimpers.

"How about we have takeout for dinner?" Steve suggests and Dexter looks happy enough. "Good lad." Dexter toddles out of the kitchen and we can hear him bounding up the stairs, letting us know that the coast is clear. "You two should sit down."

And so we do. Brodie and I sit at the island, my Aunt and Uncle on the opposite side of us. They look grave, almost like they're about to tell me that my Mum has died all over again.

"Go on, then," I prompt, growing tired of all this waiting about and dancing around points.

"That man was Tom Grayson," Steve says. "He's your father."

"I knew it!" I say.

"How do *you* know?" Debbie questions.

Shit, yeah; I only know this because of the diary which I'm not supposed to have.

"Just a guess," I shrug. "Steve looked like he knew who he was. Who else could he be?"

"Right," Debbie says, not entirely convinced. "If he's after you, it's not for good reasons."

"No shit!" I complain. "Look, you just need to be honest with me about all of this. If I'm in danger, then I want to know why."

"We should call the police," Steve says to Debbie.

"Helloooooo?" I say, waving my hand about in front of them.

"Gracie!" Debbie shouts. I don't think I've ever seen her look so stressed before. "Leave it."

And I'm quiet.

I look at Brodie. He seems just as confused as me but I think he's on my side.

"I'm going to go and ring it in, have someone come over," Debbie says. "You should check the cameras."

"Cameras?" Brodie asks.

"And then we can tell the police when they get here," Debbie continues. And the two of them leave, Brodie and I by ourselves.

"What the actual fuck?" I ask him. He shrugs his shoulders, shaking his head.

"It's odd," he agrees. "Have you told Zoe?"

"Not yet," I say. "Why, do you think I should?"

"Isn't she your best friend?"

Is she? I've only just started considering her as a friend, let alone my favourite one. But then I realise something: Zoe is my *only* friend. Doesn't that make her the best one by default? Either way, she deserves to know what's going on.

> So, the man was in fact Tom. And Tom is in fact my dad.

> We're back home now.

> Debbie is calling the police and Steve is 'checking the cameras'.

I don't expect a reply straight away but at least it's done; she knows just as much as Brodie and I now, the three of us somehow in this weird mess together.

"Do you want to read a diary entry now?" Brodie suggests.

It's a little risky; I don't know how long Debbie and Steve will be but I'm just itching to know what happened next.

"Quickly," I say. I put the vinyl bag on the counter and slide the diary out onto my lap. "Read it here."

He nods and the two of us skim over the next bit.

15th September 2001

Dear Diary,

Well, it's official. I'm going to keep the baby. I told my parents and they were angry (you've no idea - they were shouting around the house for days, angry at how I've let them all down and caused embarrassment for the family). Mum was adamant at first that I should get rid of it but she and Dad had a private conversation. Ever since then, abortion hasn't even been an option.

Debbie is so disappointed in me too. She thinks it will mess up my whole life and that Tom is a low life. She and Steve are going to stay here for a while with their new baby, Brodie, to help out with everything. She will be rubbing that in my face too; she waited until the 'proper age' to have a child. I don't care what she thinks, though. I might not like how Tom is handling any of this but

I just couldn't kill my baby. That's how it would have felt... Whatever happens, I will be there for them and love them in a way my parents can never love me.

That's not to say that Tom has got off lightly, by the way. He's in just as much trouble as me, probably even more. My parents had his over to discuss it; he couldn't ignore me now. I naively thought it would sort everything out but Tom was so mad at me...

"It was one time!" he'd said in front of everyone. I was red in the face, terrified of what everyone was thinking. "It's her fault, not mine."

"But did you use protection?" his Dad asked, again with an audience. Why did this all have to be happening out in the open? Tom and I should have been able to discuss it maturely by ourselves.

"No," he'd shuffled.

"Well, there's fifty percent of the blame to you, then," his Dad had said, leaning back on the sofa like he was done with it all.

"Hang on a second," my Mum had said, looking all confused. "Does that mean that if he'd worn a condom and she'd got pregnant, it would have been all Eve's fault? That's not how it works."

And then she just kept going. It turned into a full on shouting match and I just sat there, hands under my legs on the sofa, watching it all unfurl. I have never felt so alone before. But I found a little bit of comfort in knowing that I am growing a tiny little baby inside of me.

I will never feel alone again now that I'm a mother. And I am going to do my best by my child, as much as I can, whether Tom helps out or not. If I'm honest, I don't think I want him to be around at all. Once upon a time, I think I liked him. But now that I know him... well, he's not exactly father material.

I'll write soon. There's a lot do, though.

Eve

"Wow," I whisper, looking at my cousin. He's staring at me too, concern in his eyes. "That was…"

"A lot," he finishes for me. And just in time too. "Police are on their way," Debbie says, coming back into the kitchen. I snap the diary shut and slide it back into my bag, letting it slither to the floor. "What are you two up to?" she adds, peering at us both suspiciously.

"Just chatting," I say.

"I thought you didn't like him," she replies.

"He's growing on me," I shrug. "Anyways, you promised takeout."

"Later," she says. "We need to sort this stuff out first. I'm going to go help Steve; listen out for the door and only answer it if it's the police, okay?"

"Yeah," Brodie agrees.

But my Aunt is still looking at me; out of both of us, I'm the one who is most likely to ignore her instructions.

"I won't," I tell her.

"Good," she says. "This is serious." And then she turns on her heel, leaving us again.

"They're being so odd," Brodie says. "It's actually freaking me out a bit."

"You're freaked out?" I spit. "My Mum might have been *murdered* and the psychopath who did it is following me." Before he can even defend himself, though, my phone dings.

> Well that's an update and a half! How are u feeling?

> Honestly?

> Fucking scared.

> It will be okay! Do u want me to come over? Am I allowed?

> I don't think they will let you... but maybe I can sneak u in tonight?

> I'll let you know.

> Okay!!! Good luck, Gracie <333

Maybe I have been too harsh about her. She's spent so much of her time trying to help me recently but I've been trying to hold her at arm's length. I know why I'm doing it but I'm starting to think that maybe I shouldn't be... maybe I don't *need* to.

And then there's a knock on the door. Three loud taps.

The police are here.

Twenty

Brodie stands up first to answer the door but I don't want to be left by myself; any independence that I had before has vanished now that I feel like I'm going to choke on my own stomach. So I go with him, the two of us traipsing down the hallway up to the front door.

"Who is it?" Brodie asks. We listen for the answer.

"Police," comes the reply.

Brodie and I look at each other; do we trust that it's the truth? I realise we don't when he peeks through the spy glass to check, giving me a small nod of approval to me before opening the door.

"We had a call from a Debbie Granger," one of them says. They're both kitted out in full uniform, one a man and the other a woman, each one looking serious.

"Yes, that's my Mum," Brodie says, opening the door wider. "Come in."

They step inside and Brodie locks up the door straight away, not even bothering to look outside for any lurking stalkers.

"Ah, you're here," Debbie says, coming from the office with Steve behind her. "Shall we go into the living room?" She guides us all through the hall and we take a seat. I stick close to Brodie; for once, I actually want him around. I'm so tired of being alone; I wasn't little miss popular before my Mum's death but I wasn't by myself all the time either. I'm starting to miss that.

"Can I get you any drinks?" Debbie offers.

"No, thank you," the man says. "I'm PC Clarke and this is PC Blake. We've not had chance to go over the original files since we came here straight away but as the last update was only a year ago, we know the vast majority."

What does he mean by the *last* update? Has all of this been going on longer than Mum's death?

"Yes," Debbie replies. "We didn't expect him to be back so soon."

Back so soon? I'm literally shaking while listening, trying to make sense of it all.

"Okay, so which of you saw him today?" PC Clarke asks, bringing out a little notepad and pen to jot down my newly-acquired trauma.

"Everyone except for me," Debbie says. "I was at home while they were in York for the day."

"Right," he says, already writing something down. Seriously, what is there to write down already? "Okay, so, Gracie, is it?" He looks at me and I freeze for a moment.

"Yes," I reply, looking at Debbie for help. I don't know what she can do; she doesn't do a whole lot to help me.

"Could you walk me through what happened earlier today? And make sure you give lots of detail."

"Uhm, sure," I stumble. "Well, the first time I was in a coffee shop. That little independent one down North Street. He came up to me and asked if I was meeting anyone."

"And why do you think he did that?" he says, not even looking up from his paper as he scribbles it all down.

"I don't know," I reply truthfully. "Maybe because he couldn't do anything if I was meeting someone."

"Yes, yes, that's good," he says. "Go on."

"And then he left, looking kind of annoyed," I remember. "Uhm but then I left because I didn't really want to stick around in case he came back. I went to the record store and he came in and spoke to me again. He said that she deserved it."

"Who deserved what?" PC Clarke asks.

"I don't know," I admit, feeling completely useless. "But then he left and I called Steve to come and meet me."

The rest of the interview continues in the same way; me giving a bit of an explanation and PC Bossy Boots cutting in with questions that I either don't know the answers to or would literally be able to answer if he just listened. But when we get to the end, it feels like a massive relief. Reliving it was almost as scary as going through it the first time.

"That's everything we need from you, thank you," he says. "We'd like to speak to Debbie and Steve alone now."

"But it's not about them," I say. Why am I being pushed aside again and what the actual fuck is going on? "I'm the one who was followed. He's *my* Dad."

"There's a lot more to this than you think, Gracie," PC Clarke says. "It's best to do this the proper way to keep things running smoothly. If we need you, we will call you down again."

I look at my Aunt, hoping she will say something so that I can stay. But she wants me gone just as much as the police do. So then I try Brodie; surely after everything he would stand up for me? But he nods his head towards the corridor, begging me to go with him, and I'm stuck. I can't do anything about it and it's killing me. Once again, I have to just sit back and watch all the awful stuff happening around me.

Once we're out in the hallway, I whisper at Brodie furiously.

"What are you doing?"

"There was no point arguing," he says back. "Especially when we can just listen in from out here."

"Ohhh," I say, a small smile creeping onto my lips. "Alright, alright, I like this."

I press my ear against the door, trying to hear anything, but it's so muffled that I can't make out a single word.

"This is not going to work," I tell him.

"We'll just have to try something else," he says. "Come with me."

I follow him up the stairs and grimace when he leads us into his room. I make a habit out of avoiding it, terrified that it will have the smell of a stereotypical teenage boy bedroom. But surprisingly, it's tidier than mine. I close the door behind me and watch as he logs onto his computer.

"What are you doing?" I ask curiously.

"Hacking into Dad's phone," he says as though it's a very normal thing to do. "We can hijack the sound and listen to anything his phone can hear.

"Let's hope he's got it on him," I sigh.

"It's always in his back right pocket," Brodie says. "He never leaves it anywhere; he's weirdly attached to it."

"Works for us, though," I say. "Oh my God, that looks so confusing." He's pulled up some kind of programme that has a bunch of strange graphics across it.

"Luckily, it's not difficult for me," he says, sliding his headphones on and passing me another pair. "I've got a dual connector; we can't listen to this out loud and risk them hearing it."

"Fairs," I say, taking the headset and putting it on. At first, there's a fluffy sound but I'm unable to make anything out. But then, as he begins to meddle with the buttons on the screen, the words come more into focus and I can hear everyone's voices as though I am still downstairs with them. "That's insane."

"I have my talents," he says. "Now, listen."

And I do. I listen to every word that is said, trying to take it all in and piece the different parts together.

"Just to confirm, the last issue was a year ago when Eve Myers was killed?" PC Clarke asks.

"Yes," Debbie answers. "They couldn't confirm that it was him who killed her so he was written off as innocent."

"But you still believe it was him?"

"Yes."

"Right. What happened today means that the case will be kick started again; there is new evidence now."

"Good, good."

"Gracie may need to be updated on everything that has happened," the officer says, finally understanding that I should be clued in. "It's probably best to do it down at the station and we can get a formal statement from her."

"She gave one after Eve died," Debbie reminds him.

"Yes but that was when it was all considered an accident," is the reply.

I hold my breath, scared to make a single sound and miss anything; this next part feels important.

"If this becomes a murder case, Gracie is going to be a key figure in it. You can't keep protecting her, even though she might not want to hear it all."

I slide the headphones off.

"I knew that they were keeping things from me," I say. "I just knew it."

"But not in a mean way," Brodie replies, standing up for his parents. "The officer just said they've been trying to protect you. They thought it was for the best."

"Do I look like I'm okay, though?"

"It's a tough situation," he says. "At least you've got the diary."

"The diary…" It's still downstairs in the kitchen, tucked against the island counter where I left it. I hope they don't go through my bag. But I don't have to worry for very long; there's a knock on Brodie's door before it swings open. It's Steve.

"The police are leaving, now," he says. "How are you both?"

"Just fab," I say, folding my arms.

"Look, Gracie," he says.

But I turn away from him. I'm not giving him any chances to worm his way out of this. If they had been lying about a small thing, it wouldn't matter. But this is huge; this is quite literally a life and death situation in that I'm alive while my own Mum is dead. I should have been way more involved than they've let me be; I should have been at the centre of it all, finding out who is responsible for driving into her, for taking her life. But like always, my feelings weren't even considered.

This is why I'm better off alone. People are either taken from you or they just leave you. There's no in between. No other option.

Twenty One

I'm forced to go downstairs for tea once the promised pizza is ordered but I refuse to say a single word. I head straight to get my bag with her diary in and the carrier with the vinyl, taking them upstairs and hiding them under my bed. Moving them was the only thing that I could think about but now that it's done, I reluctantly head back down and sit at the dining table beside Brodie: my usual spot. We exchange a look, both of us knowing that we can't talk about all the things we want to out loud.

The doorbell rings, giving us a moment of privacy as Debbie and Steve go to collect it. Only Dexter is left behind but he's so preoccupied with his Pokémon level to care.

"Why haven't they said anything about how I'll have to go to the station?" I say frantically.

"I don't know," Brodie shakes his head. "They probably don't want you to worry."

"I wish I could trust that," I say, rolling my eyes. But then, before I can complain anymore, the pizza boxes and sides are placed on the table, Dexter abandoning his game as soon as he smells it.

"Tuck in," Debbie says as she and Steve sit down too.

I open up one of the boxes, taking two slices of pepperoni pizza and dumping it on my plate. I'll happily eat the takeout but I'm not giving in and playing family with them. They had their chance; they should have been honest with me from the start instead of being sneaky and lying.

My phone buzzes in my pocket.

"You can check it after tea," Debbie warns me. "You know the rules."

"You also teach your kids that lying is bad," I mutter, not even regretting it. If they're going to play games, then I'll just have to join in.

"That's enough," Debbie says but even she looks like she has no idea what she's saying. Is that a little hint of guilt in the corner of her eye? I doubt it; she's a witch and not the good kind. "Just eat your pizza; takeout is expensive."

"You bought Brodie a car," I remind them. "I think you can afford a pizza."

This time, Debbie doesn't bother to reply to me with words. Instead, she looks at me with that pitiful look she had at the memorial before dropping her eyes back to her food. Hmm. I guess she doesn't want to start anything, probably because Dexter is here. Or, maybe because she knows I'm right in all of this; I shouldn't have been lied to about something that is potentially putting me in danger. It's common sense. How is keeping me ignorant classed as protective? News flash; it's not.

So I eat my food in silence and, as soon as I'm finished, I try to find my escape.

"I'm done," I say. "Can I go now?"

Debbie and Steve glance at one another again, talking with their eyes. I'm getting really tired of them doing that. They're married, not telepathic.

"Sure," Debbie answers. "But Steve is taking you down to the station in the morning. They need to ask you a few more questions about what happened today."

Now is the time to put on my best poker face and pretend that I've got no idea what they're talking about.

"What?" I say in the most gormless manner I can.

"It's just procedure," Steve cuts in. "Nothing to worry about."

I narrow my eyes at them; they're not fooling me.

"Cool, what time?" I reply, clearly trying to hurry the conversation along.

"Nine," he tells me.

Great, another early start.

"See you then," I say and I head upstairs, not bothering to wait for a response or thank them for the pizza. They've got a lot more grovelling to do before I'm going to forgive them for what they've kept from me. Besides, they haven't even bothered to apologise yet; they still think that they're in the right.

I'll be angry at them later, though. For now, there's only one thing on my mind. As soon as I'm in my bedroom, I get out my phone to check what the notification had been; my guess was right.

> U okay? xx
>
> I can come whenever

As usual, I fall into the 'should I' kind of state, wondering if I feel safe enough to let her in. Not into the house but into my life, into my close circle. I don't really have a circle, though; it's more of a line. A very straight and short one. But I *want* to message her back... I want her to be involved.

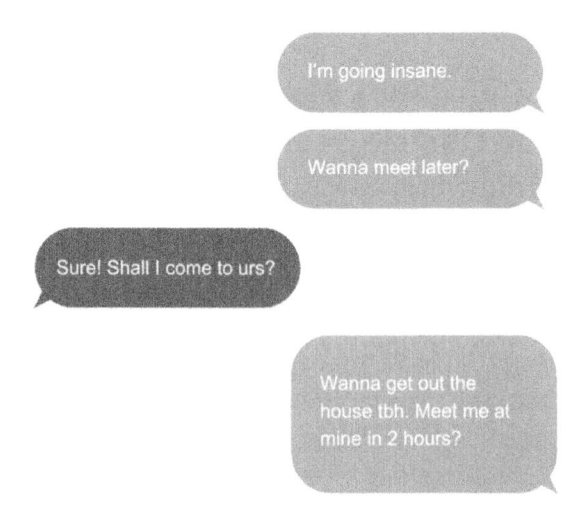

> I'm going insane.
>
> Wanna meet later?
>
> Sure! Shall I come to urs?
>
> Wanna get out the house tbh. Meet me at mine in 2 hours?

> I'll be there xx

You'd think I'd want to stay far away from the outside world and keep myself safe behind a locked door. But how am I going to find out anything from here? And how would I sneak Zoe in when they're all over me like hawks now? I'll wait for them to go to bed and then I'll climb out the window, down the trellis and figure everything out.

But there's something else I have to do.

> Wanna come out with Zoe and I tonight? Gonna do some digging.

Surprisingly, Brodie replies quickly.

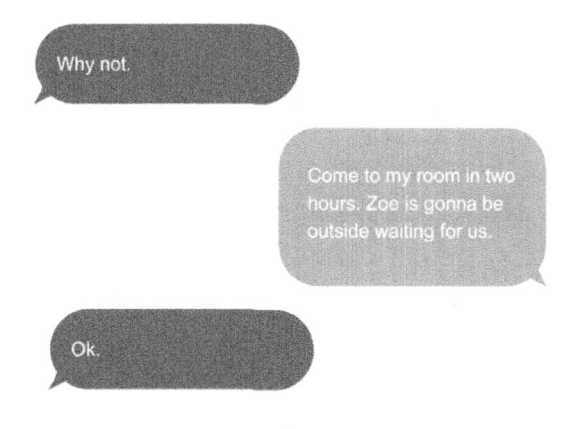

> Why not.

> Come to my room in two hours. Zoe is gonna be outside waiting for us.

> Ok.

It's a dry reply but he's also still downstairs with everyone; I haven't heard anyone's footsteps on the stairs yet. But I'll take it. Having Brodie there might deter Tom from trying anything if he decides to turn up; three is a lot more intimidating than two.

...

The hours pass slowly; I'm itching to read more of Mum's diary but I also want to wait for Zoe and Brodie so that I don't have to be alone. The things that she is writing about are, emotionally, a lot. It's even harder to read when the memories belong to your own Mum who was most likely murdered. I always knew that there was something off about it all but I couldn't have ever guessed this. Why is Tom so angry with her? And why is he following me now? I've never even met him so how could *I* have done anything?

My phone buzzes, distracting me from my thoughts. It's Zoe.

> I'm outside! Hiding beside ur house though cos it's spooky now.

> Yeah, Brodie should be here any sec and we will come down.

Hopefully, she won't mind him coming.

And then, just like clockwork, my door opens quietly; Brodie slides his body through the small gap.

"You could have just opened it normally, doofus," I say to him in a whisper.

"I'm not taking risks," he says. "You ready? Is Zoe here?"

"Just outside," I tell him, picking up my backpack which has Mum's diary already safely in. There's no way I am forgetting to bring that. "Let's go."

And I climb through the window (not very gracefully) and tiptoe down the trellis, jumping the last few feet onto the drive.

"You okay?" I say to Zoe; she looks relieved to see me as she nods with a smile.

Then Brodie begins his descent, shutting the window just enough so that we will be able to get back in later on. He's the worst out of all three of us at coming down, his shoes not wedging into the empty spots correctly. We're just lucky that he's not making noise while he struggles; Debbie and Steve would kill us if they could see us now.

"That was awful," he says, looking at me like it's my fault he's terrible at climbing.

"Where are we going?" Zoe asks. She really wants to get out of here and after today, I don't blame her. I don't exactly want to be hanging about in the darkness either.

"Maybe the amusements? We can sit at the diner in there and there will be people about," I suggest.

"Works for me," Zoe says.

"Yeah," Brodie agrees.

And so we head into town, hoping that we won't walk past anyone that would grass us up to Debbie and Steve for being out. But no one knows that I'm grounded, after all. Why on earth would they feel the need to mention it to them that they simply saw us? They just wouldn't, small town or not.

Twenty Two

The amusements are surprisingly busy. I guess it is a Saturday night but it's such a dead town usually at this time of the year. It's normally only like this over the summer months when the tourists flock in to have their seaside holiday. But somehow, there are a bunch of people here, trying their luck at the 2p machines and the bingo like they're actually going to win something.

I haven't been here in years.

When I was little, my grandma would bring me down when my Mum needed her to look after me. She'd only let me have a quid, otherwise I'd just be wasting her money, but I cherished it so much. I'd have to get it changed into coppers first and I loved watching all of the coins fall into my little tub as they spurted out of the machine. Unfortunately, I usually spent through it pretty quickly and we were never there for long. I was hurried away to do something that grandma preferred.

As she got older, she got grouchier, refusing to spend any unnecessary money. I honestly think it's the real reason that she didn't want to look after me. Obviously, being ill was part of it, but I was a burden before that too. She's old and living on a pension; I was an extra person to worry about.

But the thing is, I understand that completely. I just wish that she had been nicer about it all, especially since I'd just lost my Mum. But no, she didn't think about my feelings at all.

"There's a free booth over there," Brodie shouts over the noise, pointing towards some seats in the corner of the diner section. We head on over quickly, Zoe and I sliding in next to each other and Brodie opposite us. I take a menu from the centre and start flicking through it. I can still feel the pizza and chips in my stomach from earlier so the idea of having a full meal is a little much.

"What about ice-cream?" I suggest.

"Sounds good," Zoe replies. "I love their chocolate fudge."

"Me too!" Brodie agrees excitedly.

"How about we get a large one to split?" I ask, looking at the price of an individual one. The plan is set and Brodie goes away to place the order, returning back once it's all paid for.

"So, what are we going to do?" he asks.

"I think we should read the next entry," I sigh. "I'm nervous to but I think there might be something in there to make all of this make sense; a missing piece to the puzzle, so to speak."

"The last entry was just before her death, right?" Zoe asks and I nod. "Surely she will start to explain it all, then? Everything in there so far has been about Tom in some way. She wouldn't leave it out; it's the one place that she's been honest about it all."

She's got a good point. The likelihood of finding out what we need to know is incredibly high, it's just hard to read through. Every diary entry is another chance for me to see how much pain she was in back then; the thought that it lasted pretty much my whole life is awful. Something tells me it won't become lighter the more I read on.

"Right," I say, opening the diary to the next page. "Let's see if we can get through the next one before our ice-cream arrives."

5th November 2001

Dear Diary,

My baby bump has started to show and it's causing so much trouble. We've been able to keep it on the down low for a while, only mine and Tom's family knowing, but somehow it's got out. I've been careful. I'm always wearing baggy jumpers and doing all the same things as I did before. But then a rumour started.

It spread around school first, the entire sixth form looking at me with judgmental faces as though they have the slightest idea of how it happened. I could hear people whispering right in front of me to their friends! Do they not realise how rude and hurtful that is? Mum says that I deserve it but she's not like that when we're out in public; she tells them that it's rude to be so concerned with a teenager who's got nothing to do with them. So, I'm not really sure how she's feeling about it all.

I'll be finding out if the baby is a girl or a boy soon... I'm so excited but also extremely nervous. I think I'm having a little girl; I can just feel it. But no matter who they are, I'm going to love them so much. I'll give them the life that I never had and make sure that they're safe and free to be whatever they want to be.

I've got to go shopping with my Mum now. She refuses to let me be by myself at any point; I don't know if it's to keep me safe or to stop me from making anymore 'mistakes'.

Eve

"So, Tom took a bit of a backseat during her pregnancy," Zoe says, summarising everything we've just read. "And Eve felt alone throughout it all, like no one understood her."

It's eerily weird how I feel just like that now, only for such different reasons. And, do you know what's worse? I can do something about my situation; Eve Myers will be six feet underground for the rest of time, unable to change her narrative. That's why I have to do something about it; I have to make sure that she's remembered properly, that everyone knows the truth.

"A large chocolate fudge ice-cream with three spoons," the waiter says, bringing over a large glass bowl of ice-cream. It looks monstrous in size but I reckon the three of us will make light work of it.

"Thank you," we all chime out.

"So, do we read the next entry?" Zoe asks me. And that's when I realise that Brodie is looking at me too; it's clearly my decision.

"Yeah, we probably should," I sigh. It's hard but I know that it's necessary.

12th November 2001

Dear Diary,

So, it's official... I'm having a little girl! Tom had practically been forced by his parents to come to the hospital with us all; he looked so embarrassed. I just felt ashamed. All he'd wanted from me was a good time, yet now he's been bound to another little human for the rest of his life. I get why he wanted me to have the abortion but I just couldn't do that to her... When it came down to it, it didn't even feel like an option. But to Tom... he looks at me with such anger in his eyes, like it's my fault.

I guess it is.

But it doesn't matter because I've got my little girl and he can't take her away from me! We've pretty much all decided that I'll have her with me but he's allowed to see her. His parents expect him to; they say all his wages will have to go towards taking care of her. He was so annoyed about that. He said that I should get a job if I need money. Is he forgetting that I'm still in full time education AND pregnant?

I don't know what I ever saw in him. But I feel like I've grown up a lot since all of this began. I'm no longer the naive seventeen year old who'd had sex with a guy she barely knew because he wanted her to. I'm eighteen now... a Mum. Everything is different, even though I'm in the same town.

I won't be here long, though.

Eve

"What do you think she means by that?" Brodie asks. "It's a bit of an ominous way to end it."

"Not when you realise that she knew; she never expected anyone else to read it so she wouldn't have filled in the gaps," I say, picturing a younger version of my Mum, her stomach bulging with my tiny body. "She sounds like she wanted it, though. She *wanted* to leave."

"I don't blame her," Zoe says. "She's barely said one nice thing about her life so far."

"Except for you, Gracie," Brodie nods to me.

It's true. I'm the one thing in all of these entries that she seems happy about. That she *wants*, even if I wasn't supposed to exist in the first place. It's starting to make sense about why she lied; Green Haven was probably her escape from it all.

"Guys," Brodie whispers, suddenly making my heart fall from my chest. I look up at him slowly, scared about what he will say next. "We've got a friend." His head nods ever so softly, pointing behind Zoe and I. He doesn't have to say who it is; we're all wildly aware that Tom is here, most likely following us. I can't be surprised. This is a public place; he can scare me all he wants but he can't actually do anything.

"Relax," I say.

"Are you crazy?" Zoe says, looking at me like I really am.

"He's all talk at the moment," I remind them. "Besides, there are people everywhere. Is he really going to try something?"

"Maybe if he's fucking looney! Duck!" Brodie shouts. Not sure why, Zoe and I throw ourselves down, hovering underneath the table in the same way we'd hidden in his car not long ago. There's a loud thump above us, rattling the table legs.

"What the fuck?" I shout.

"That was a rounder's bat," Brodie explains. "That he just threw across the room aiming at your head."

"What was that about 'all talk'?" Zoe says, shaking.

"Right, okay," I breathe. "Slight update, I guess?"

"You *guess*?" Brodie says before another shot is taken, this time missing the table and landing beside us. There are screams now, running footsteps and shouts of fear.

And we're stuck.

Tom has us well and truly trapped.

Twenty Three

I never thought I would feel this kind of fear again after my Mum died. Racing through the hospital corridors to find her connected to all of those tubes is an image I'll never forget but I had no idea the chain of events that would unfold after it all ended. Who would have predicted that I'd be at my local amusements with a cousin that I hated and a friend I never thought I'd make, all three of us hiding underneath a piece of plastic because my secret Dad has decided to lob sports equipment at us? Not me.

"What do we do?" I say.

An alarm sounds then, ringing around us all and making my ears go all funny.

"Looks like the staff are on it," Brodie says but I don't feel so sure. No one knows that we're under here... except for Tom. "Maybe one of us should take a look?"

Zoe and I stare him down; he's the oldest, after all.

"If I die, it's on you," he says, crawling out cautiously. He looks in the direction where the bat had come from first and then the other way before sliding out. "I think the alarm scared him off. You can come out."

I don't feel fully safe to but I also can't hide under the table for the rest of the night. Zoe holds out her hand to me and I take it without hesitation; she's proved herself over and over to me. I need to let go of my fear, especially when there are bigger things to be scared of... Maybe being vulnerable is okay in some situations.

Once we're out in the open, the amusements are nearly deserted, save for a few staff members and ourselves.

"Do we go?" I ask uselessly; I don't think any of us have the faintest idea what you're supposed to do in these scenarios. I shouldn't have even been here in the first place but I just had to get out of there... I had to figure it all out. I might be going to the station in the morning but who's to say they're going to tell me everything? They could just feed me the important bits so that they can weasel as much information out of me as possible.

For a murder case about MY Mum. Who was supposedly killed by MY Dad. Yet I'm the one fumbling in the dark like a fool. It's not fair, not at all.

"Call the police?" Brodie suggests.

"And have them grass on us to Debbie and Steve? Fat chance," I say. "We'll just have to get home quickly. Zoe, will you be okay?" She looks terrified at the idea of going out into the night alone. "Okay, new plan: Brodie and I will walk you home. That way, no one is alone at any point."

"Thanks," she says gratefully and I know for certain that I've made the right choice, even if it means I'll have to be outside for longer. But I can't send her into danger... not now that I care about her.

I put Mum's diary into my bag and look at the sad piece of ice-cream we only half ate. I have a feeling that it won't be my biggest problem... I don't know what has sparked Tom's recent anger with me but I doubt it's going away any time soon.

…

Luckily, Zoe only lives a few streets down from Debbie's house and so we're on the road to safety soon enough. I'm more aware than before, looking all around me for any sign of insane men carrying baseball bats. Although, I'd be surprised if he had any more on him; two is already a little overboard if you ask me.

"Tonight was a little chaotic," I say, kicking a newspaper with my shoe as we turn onto our street.

"I'm starting to wish I'd just stayed in and played my video game," Brodie says but I think I know him well enough now to see that he's just playing around. One little glance at him and he's got a tiny little smile there that proves my hypothesis. "I really hope that some of your questions are answered tomorrow, Gracie."

"And I really hope that the event at the amusements doesn't go semi viral with our faces on

CCTV footage," I reply. "Let's agree not to tell Debbie and Steve - or the police - what happened tonight. It will just make things worse and things are already awful."

"I don't know Gracie," he says, looking unsure. "This is serious... he's gone from following you to attacking you within the space of a day. That's quite drastic."

"I know," I say. "I know. But I just, I don't know... I have a feeling."

"So you know but you don't know?"

I glare at him.

"This is bigger than you think." He phrases it like a warning; like we're back to our old ways of hating each other.

"It's about me," I remind him. "Not you."

"I never said it was," he says. "But you need to think about this. I think you should bring the diary with you to the station tomorrow; tell them you think it's important, about how it's got loads about Tom in there. You go on about justice but don't you see it? This might be the answer to getting that. You want answers, right?" I nod my head reluctantly. "What's the use in you knowing if the whole world doesn't?"

"I just want her to be remembered properly," I whisper, tears brimming in my eyes. I feel like I've let her down, like I should be so much better at all of this. Stronger.

"Discovering her killer and putting him behind bars will mean that," he says. "Otherwise, he gets off scot-free for murder."

Murder. The word is harsh but most likely true; the police might not have been able to prove it all this time, yet I'm pretty sure it's their theory. So why has he been left to roam the streets ever since? It's the lack of evidence, it has to be.

"Okay," I agree. "I'll give them the diary." I'm not sure about it, doubt is coursing through every inch of me right now, but I think that Brodie is right. I don't want Tom to win... to have all the power. To have gotten away with killing the most important person in my life who didn't deserve any of it. He was awful to her before I was even born; I still don't understand how he could stoop so close to Hell as to *kill* a person, though. It's so messed up... *he's* messed up.

"It's the right choice," Brodie says in a whisper. We've just reached the drive and, as of yet, there's no stalker in sight.

"Your parents are going to kill both of us when they find out," I reply, remembering how Brodie made me promise not tell anyone he had given me the box of her things. It feels like forever ago now and it's barely been any time at all... so much has happened. It's become heavy.

"Well, this is more important."

I think this is the most I've ever liked him. It's like I've finally felt understood by him, like he's being serious and realises what all this is for. I know that he's probably felt this way all along but it's the first time he's said it, word for word, out loud.

"Thanks, Brodie," I say; the tears in my eyes aren't all bad now.

"Now, how are we going to climb up this trellis?" he asks, ignoring how I'm crying like he knows I want him to. "Something tells me that it's going to be a lot harder this way up."

"Follow after me," I say, wiping at my eyes with my sleeve.

Brodie is correct; the journey back up is definitely harder than the original one coming down but it's far from impossible. It takes a few minutes for us both to navigate our way up silently and I'm relieved when my feet are back on the ground.

"So, what now?" I ask, closing the window.

"I guess we go to bed," he says. It feels like such a mundane thing after everything that just happened but he's right. It's the logical thing to do, the only thing to do.

"Right, well, I guess I'll see you tomorrow," I reply. "Thanks for coming."

"No worries, Gracie." And he's gone, leaving me alone to think about the mess that I've been dealt.

Twenty Four

The morning feels like absolute hell as I turn over to turn off my alarm. It's far too early to be awake, especially since I practically got zero sleep. I was tossing and turning to the extent that I actually banged my head on my bedside table at one point. Half asleep, I barely processed it at the time but now that I'm awake, I can feel a pulse grating against the spot.

Deciding that there's no point in putting off the inevitable, I leave my bed as quickly as possible, readying myself for the day. Already, I can picture Debbie complaining about whatever I wear; she will say that this is important and I need to dress suitably so I don't make a bad impression. I'm sorry? I'm not the murderer here. I'm not the psycho ex boyfriend who still has a grudge sixteen years later. I wasn't even alive when this whole thing began, for fuck's sake.

"You ready?" There's a knock on my door at the same time that Steve speaks through the wood.

"Nearly," I shout back, combing my hair so that it isn't a complete frizz ball. Sometimes I wish that I looked pretty; I know I never will be in the generic sense but I always hope that someone will at least look at me and think 'wow, she's got style'. I try so hard to be my own person; my Mum always taught me that it was the most important thing, that no one could ever take it away from you.

Well. They did.

Because no one knows the real reason that Eve Myers is no longer behind the counter in her flower shop, smiling at the usual customers and spending time with her daughter.

But Tom knows.

I pick up my bag from last night, feeling the weight of her diary in there. Am I really going to pass it over as evidence? Do I even trust the police? I feel like it's so damn obvious that it wasn't an accident, especially after yesterday. The man practically admitted to it with his whole 'she deserved it' act. Why can't they just arrest him and declare it how it is: Ever Myers was murdered.

Obviously, I'd rather she not be dead at all but I can't change that. All I can do it get the truth out there, even if means accepting what happened is more gruesome and messed up than I once imagined. She deserves that.

Before I can leave, there's something itching at me to read another entry. In a few hours, it won't be mine anymore; I won't be able to read through it and feel close to her. I'll be giving away control too, passing over a vital piece of the puzzle for *other* people to figure out what to do with it.

And so I slide out the notebook and curl up on the bed, turning to the page we got to last night.

25th December 2001

Dear Diary,

I'm only three months away from the due date now and it's starting to feel real. Obviously, it did before too but now it's in a different way. I can feel her kicking sometimes, begging to come out and be in the world. It's a bittersweet feeling to know that she is naive to the realities on the other side of my stomach. I hope that I can keep her innocent forever but I know that this is just a silly notion; I can't protect her as much as I'd like, especially not here.

I've been thinking more and more that I might leave after she's born. This town is full of nosy people, do-gooders that don't actually care about how people feel, boys who want to have sex with you but then leave you alone with a baby.

Well, Tom's around kind of, but not by choice. His parents still force him to come to every scan and even though he will never have custody, he has to pay child support. They think it's fair but they also see it as teaching him a lesson. That feels so wrong... to treat a human being like a 'lesson'. I'm glad that I'll be a single mother. I don't want Tom anywhere near my child. The longer this goes on... the worse he is becoming. I never thought that he had it in him to become violent but he's started threatening me. Whenever we're at a scan or his family is over for dinner, he will get me alone and lean in... whispering into my ear the most awful things.

I don't want to write them down, mainly because I don't want to remember them. But they are scary. He even said that he would kill me if he needed to... so that he wouldn't have to bother with the baby. How terrible is that? Sure, I was starting to get the feeling that he was a bit of a player but a murderer? That's a whole new thing.

I'll keep you updated. I'm terrified of what he might do. I feel like I can't tell anyone. They would take one look at him behaving completely normally around everyone else and write him off doing anything truly awful. But I don't trust that they are empty threats...

Eve

It's the perfect entry to read right before going to the police station; the proof that he killed her is right there. It means that there is actually a chance of him going down for it but do I really want to leave that up to the officers? They've already wasted a year letting a guilty (and dangerous) man walk free. I pass his family garage every day for school!

So, no. I won't be giving them the diary. It's mine now and I'm certain that I need to keep a hold of it. I slide it back into my bag and hide it at the bottom of my wardrobe, tucking it behind my other pairs of shoes and underneath the hanging clothes. Unless anyone is *really* stooping, they won't find it there. Well, they better not.

I throw on my Docs and put on my jacket; as usual, I don't have time for a proper breakfast. I grab a cereal bar from the kitchen cupboard and meet Steve by the front door.

"Is it just us two?" I ask, almost hoping that he won't say yes. But he does.

I really need to talk to Brodie; I need to explain that I've changed my mind about giving them the diary. I'm not ready to let it go... to lose that connection with my Mum, especially when it's my history too. But he doesn't know and I can't help but worry that he might bring it up to someone, giving the whole thing away.

I take out my phone and drop him a message, hoping that he will be the one to see it and he won't be mad. But my hopes are dashed before I've even buckled my seatbelt.

> That is a terrible idea.

> I'll explain when I'm back.

> Just trust me, okay?

> Fine. Good luck though.

> Thanks.

I'm especially quiet in the car, basking in the rare time that I get to sit in the front seat. It's always either given to Steve (because Debbie refuses to let him drive her anywhere) or Brodie because he's the oldest which means I get lumped with Dexter. But it doesn't mean I'm happy about all of this. I suppose I should be; Mum's death is finally getting the attention it should have had a year ago but I'm just so angry. At Tom. At Debbie and Steve. The police. Mostly everyone, to be honest.

Why has it taken *this* long?

"We're here," Steve says, pulling into the car park. "You ready?"

My answer is a silent stare of 'what do you think?'

"Look," he sighs. "I know it's not easy."

"You reckon?"

"But it's the only way to bring justice."

"So why are you all keeping things from me?" I question. Fuck it; I want answers and they're all pissing me off. "I know that there is more to it than what you are saying; I'm not five."

He looks down at the steering wheel, bracing his hands on it.

"It's never been our place to say," he says. "I'm sure the police will have decided what you need to know and they will tell you today. But we were given explicit orders by them after your Mum died to not tell you certain things. If you found out, it would have changed everything... maybe stopping them from being able to charge him with anything."

"They know?" Realisation creeps over me. "The police *know* that Tom killed her?"

His delayed response tells me everything I need to know.

"They've always been *almost* certain," he says. "But there wasn't any actual evidence, nothing to really prove it. So, we've all had to play the long game, hoping that he would do something to give it away or that new evidence would come to light."

I think about the diary at the back of my wardrobe with guilt.

"Yesterday might have been traumatic for you," he continues. "But it means something. Eve might finally be able to rest in peace."

"You actually cared about her, didn't you?" I ask, though it's not really a question. I've thought all this time that he and Debbie didn't give two hoots about my Mum but maybe I've been wrong. Perhaps they really were just trying to protect me all along, saving me from the same fate.

"She was more than a sister-in-law to me," he nods. "She and Debbie had a tough relationship but this thing with Tom was always a thing. We both knew how hard it was for her and how much she needed a fresh start away from it all."

I can't say it out loud but that's the confirmation I needed about why she lied about Green Haven. She didn't tell me that she wasn't from there because she was desperately trying to let go one of the most awful things that a person can go through: abuse.

Twenty Five

Walking into the reception feels really odd. It's almost like I'm the one in trouble, even though the most illegal thing I've ever done is smoke a cigarette a few times. I'm glad I've left that habit behind but the distraction for it really sucks.

"Good morning," Steve says with a low voice as we walk up to the counter. "I've got Gracie Myers for a meeting."

"Thank you," the lady replies, beginning to type something onto the computer. "Yes, that's great. If you could just go through those doors and up the stairs to the second floor. There are a few chairs outside the interview room."

'Interview room' sounds deadly serious. I instantly picture those ones in films with the one way mirror and the emptiness, save for a single table and two chairs. Isn't that where the criminals are taken? I didn't do anything wrong...

"Thank you," Steve says. I follow after him as the woman buzzes us through the door, trailing up the stairs. It reminds me of yesterday, running up the stairwell, hearing Tom's footsteps below... wondering if we would make it safely to the car. I can almost hear him now, bounding behind me, getting closer and closer and...

I scream.

"Gracie?" Steve's voice echoes but I can't process where he is. I'm not really here... I'm in yesterday's memory, running from the man who killed my Mum. "Gracie? Are you okay?"

I fall flat against the wall, watching the room spin chaotically. It hurts... it hurts so bad. He's there... and he's here... and he's going to hurt me. He's going to kill me just like he killed her. Speeding down the street in his missing car. I'm flying. Falling.

Dead.

"Mum!" I wail. My body hits the floor in a lump, splayed out across multiple steps. "Mum!"

"Gracie?" Steve says. His arm goes around me, trying to be comforting. But it's sickening.

"Don't hurt me!" I squeal. Why? Just *why*. Why did Tom have to kill my Mum? Why is he after me? Why. Why. Why. Why. Why.

Black.

...

"Gracie?" It's Steve's voice again but it's clearer now.

I open my eyes, fluttering them softly until I make out where I am. I'm on a sofa, a cushion beneath my head and a blanket over my body. The room is warm and cosy, decorated almost like a home, except it's more like Debbie and Steve's house than my own back in Green Haven. This one doesn't look lived in; there's no clutter. Only purposeful decoration.

"What happened?" I ask, sitting up. Steve is beside me, looking more concerned that he had been yesterday, and the two officers that had come to ours are sat opposite us on another sofa. Okay, this is a little embarrassing.

"You had a panic attack," PC Clarke explains. "In the stairwell. Do you remember?"

I think as hard as I can. There is a slight hint of it in my memory but nothing exact.

"Bits of it."

"Good, good," he replies. "Now, we do need to go over some things with you today. They might be triggering for you; do you feel well enough to help us with them?"

"Will it help my Mum?" I ask.

"Yes," is the answer.

I might not want to give them the diary but I can give them bits of information; enough to put him behind bars for life hopefully.

"Perfect," he answers with a slight smile. "We do have to record everything that is said in this room. Is that okay with you?"

"Yeah," I answer; I don't really have a choice, do I?

"Great," he says. PC Blake switches on a little machine on the coffee table between us that is obviously the recorder. That means this is real now;

there is no backing out. "This is PC Clarke, collar number 4309."

"And PC Blake, collar number 7982."

"The date is 12.12.17," he continues, his voice monotone. "We are here to interview Grace Myers and she is accompanied by her Uncle, Steve Granger, to discuss the case of Eve Myers, case number 210945."

My heartbeats are soft but loud, pulsing in my head quietly.

"So, to begin with, we need to fill you in on a few details, Gracie," he continues. "If you need a break at any moment, please do let us know."

I nod.

"We believe that your mother was killed on purpose by Tom Grayson, your biological father."

Hearing them say it feels like I'm learning it for the first time all over again.

"We suspected him early on in the investigation but he had an alibi and there was a lack of evidence for us to convict him of any crime or even hold a trial," he explains. "This is very rare for cases like this so it did leave us a little stumped. We all agreed that the best way forward was to keep the case on the down low, letting Tom think that we were no longer onto him. In the meantime, we have been collecting things against him, building towards a trial."

Okay... this is all starting to add up... it's making some level of sense.

"Yesterday really catapulted things," he says. "We contacted the record store and they sent over the CCTV this morning for us. We have the words he said to you on video."

"About how my Mum deserved it?" I ask.

"Yes," he says. "But the problem is, he isn't very explicit. We know what he means but he's not entirely admitted to it. Do you see the issue?"

"Isn't it enough to take him in, though? If he's dangerous then -"

"Unfortunately, we're up to our neck already," he says. "The rules are that we have to have sound evidence."

"That's stupid," I say, forgetting that I'm supposed to be behaving right now.

"It is," he agrees. I'm shocked but still not entirely happy. The whole system sounds like a scam. "The reason we couldn't tell you any of this is because it might have thrown the whole thing off. If you knew, you might start taking things into your own hands, putting yourself into danger."

I can't even complain. As soon as I had any idea about what was going on, I did exactly that... walking directly into the firing line. I may have only noticed Tom following me yesterday but what if he's been tailing me all along? Maybe he had been watching Zoe and I when we went to the cliffs... back when we saw the initials on the tree.

Hang on a second. Why were their initials there if they never even dated? There was no 'happy love story' before the tragedy. It started bad and then it just got worse. Was it just my Mum who had etched the letters in, manifesting him liking her back? Maybe it was a different Eve and Tom; they're not exactly uncommon names. How much of what I thought I knew isn't even true?

Do I even know my Mum?

"But now that Tom has broken his restraining order -"

"HIS WHAT?" I explode. I feel like this is another thing that I definitely should have known about.

"We thought it a good precaution to have," he says. "We couldn't do much to ensure your safety but we did what we could. Eve had one against him for years; he was well aware. She filed for it after the child support payments stopped coming through. But now that he has broken it, we do have an excuse to further the investigation against him."

"He's shot himself in the foot, so to speak," the other officer adds.

"Which means that we need your help," PC Clarke says.

I'm a little annoyed that they're only including me now for selfish reasons but what can I do? Throw a tantrum? Refuse to speak?

"Over the last year, have you noticed anything strange?"

"You mean, have I seen Tom before yesterday?" I ask, rephrasing it for them.

"Yes."

"Only in his garage," I say nonchalantly. "I walk past it to get to school and back."

"That's the longer way home," Steve says, looking a little confused.

"I walk home with my friend," I say. He looks surprised; clearly, the idea of me hanging out with people is a foreign concept. "It's her route home." It's not the entire truth but it's good enough. It lets them know that I've been past the garage without lumping me into a big amount of trouble. So, I'm doing good so far.

"Has he ever looked at you? Spoken to you?"

"No," I say. "I don't really pay much attention. I just kind of look 'cos it's more interesting to nosy at than people's houses."

"Right," PC Clarke says.

Honestly, I think that's a pretty valid excuse. Teenagers get curious about things; what are they going to do about it?

"So, as far as you are aware, he hasn't made any attempt to interact with you until yesterday?"

"As far as I'm aware," I repeat his words back to him. Who knows if Tom has been lurking around corners all year, or even her whole life? I wasn't exactly looking for him so I wouldn't have noticed and I can't just come up with the memory now, filling in the gaps of things I don't know and never will.

"Okay," he replies.

I half want him to at least write something down so that he's not just staring at me but why bother? He's got everything on a recording.

"Did your Mum ever mention Tom when she was alive?"

"Not to me," I say. It's the truth. What I've read in the diary don't count... I didn't find out those things until after her death which is not what he is asking.

"Strange," he mutters.

"Is it, though?" I bite back. "If he's crazy enough to run her over, then surely she just didn't think he was worth knowing about."

"I don't think you believe that," the officer wonders.

Did I waver? Give something away? I think I've been doing a decent enough job at answering their questions without mentioning anything about the diary.

"What aren't you telling us?" His stare is fucking lethal right now, burning through my lies.

"I just don't like talking about it," I say. "It hurts."

"Maybe she could take a break," Steve suggests and thank God he does because I cannot hold this up any longer.

"Of course," PC Clarke says, turning off the recorder. "We will come back in ten minutes, is that okay?"

I nod reluctantly as they leave Steve and I alone. Though, I've watched enough detective shows to know that we're never completely alone. Whether it be CCTV, a one way mirror, or just plain listening on the other side of the door, this is far from private.

Twenty Six

"Are you okay?" Steve says once the door is closed.

Now is my time to really play this up, not that I need to pretend too much. This whole thing is making me so uncomfortable and anxious. Knowing that my Mum died is one thing but finding out all of this extra stuff is just so heavy. I'm sure that she would hate it if she were here, feeling guilty at what she has left behind. I would too, if I were her, but that doesn't mean that any of this is her fault. She may have let Tom into her life all of those years ago but she didn't understand what that would mean; she didn't realise how awful he really was, how *dangerous* he could be... She was only seventeen.

"Just fab," I whisper, barely even looking in Steve's direction. He can see it in my body language that I'm not fine and I shouldn't have to be. All of this is way more than any teenager signs up for.

"We will get it all sorted," he says, rubbing my back in a useless attempt to comfort me. "It's just going to take some time."

"Something that she didn't get because of that scumbag," I remind him.

"Well, yes," he stumbles.

"And now we're all here having a little chat about how my Mum was murdered and none of you thought to tell me," I continue.

"I can see why you're angry," he says.

"Can you, though?" I cut in. "You didn't lose your Mum to her psychopathic ex boyfriend, did you? You didn't walk around for a year in mourning, thinking she died in a tragic accident, only to find out that, hang on, no, actually, some idiot decided to run her over on *purpose*."

"I know, Gracie," he sighs, not even caring that I'm having a tantrum. "If it makes any difference, I wanted to tell you straight away."

"Then why didn't you?" I ask him in a calmer voice.

"I was advised not to," he admits. "Everyone else thought it would just cause you unnecessary stress; they thought that if you could just mourn her like this, in a less traumatic way, it might be easier for you."

"And what about when I inevitably found out that it wasn't an accident? What then? Because that happened, Steve. That happened."

"We hoped it would have been enough time for you to have processed her death," he answers. "There was no perfect way of dealing with this situation but you were underage; the ball was in our court. Maybe we chose the wrong option in not telling you but we just couldn't do it... we couldn't hurt you like that."

"But you wouldn't have been the ones doing the hurting," I say. "That would have been Tom."

"You would have been angry with us too and we wouldn't have blamed you," he continues. "You've been grieving."

"Is that why you always used to let me off for things?" Not that I need the confirmation; it's painfully obvious.

"Yes," he says. "But after the memorial service, we realised that maybe it had been the wrong approach. You were struggling, we could see it. We just didn't know what to do about it to make it all easier for you."

"So you grounded me?"

"We were trying to keep you out of serious trouble," he admits. "Besides, Debbie was distraught; she thought you ruined the service and that it was all her fault for not understanding you enough."

I blink. That's not what I thought Debbie was upset about at all. Not even close.

"We are both really sorry, for what it's worth."

"It's okay," I say, though it really isn't. I've been angry at them all for so long that it's going to take a bit more than a simple 'sorry we fucked up' from only one of them to fix things.

"Thank you," he replies. "Look, Gracie, I really need you to answer the officer's questions as well as you can. You can't leave anything out because even the smallest thing could help put this man behind bars. Without the car he used, it's difficult. But there is a chance of finding evidence strong enough to prove he would kill with intent."

I know that there is. I can picture the diary page easily, hidden in my wardrobe. But am I ready to hand it over? To lose the biggest connection I have to my Mum? I don't think I am... Does that make me a bad person?

"I am trying," I lie. "It's just weird."

"I know," he says. "You're doing a good job. We'll just get through this interview and then I'm sure they'll have a plan."

And then, almost on cue, the door swings open and the two officers are back, taking their seats on the opposite sofa as though they had never left.

"Are we ready to continue?" PC Clarke asks me, readying his finger to resume the recording, letting me know that we are going to do it whether I want to or not. And so I nod softly. "Perfect." His finger presses down and a small beep resounds from the machine. "So, continuing on, Gracie; do you have any recollection of your Mum speaking about Tom when she was alive?"

I should have known that they wouldn't skip over the question. They think I'm lying about something, or rather, they *know* that I am. But I've had time to compose myself now, to think about how to answer this in a way that means I can keep the diary a secret for a little longer.

"I didn't even know he existed," I tell them, truthfully enough. "I didn't even know who he was yesterday; I thought he was just a creep following me around."

He looks like he wants to call me out again but he can't; I haven't lied, not really.

"Okay," he reluctantly says. "Do you think that she would have had contact with him over the last few years of her life?"

"I wouldn't know," I say slowly. "She never said anything about him to me, remember?"

"Just checking."

Ah, so that was a bad attempt to catch me out, then.

"Was there anything suspicious in the months leading up to the crash?" comes the next question. What does that even mean?

"I don't think so," I answer. "Everything was just, well, normal."

"Normal? Okay, okay. And do you think that Tom has anything personal against your Mum? Something that would make him act violently towards her?"

My eyes are starting to tear up a little bit now as I think about it all. I'd love to say that it feels surreal but the truth of it is, it feels more real now than it ever has before.

"Other than the obvious?" I say; it's my cop-out answer to play on what they already know.

"Yes, other than that," he confirms for me.
"No, then," I reply simply. "I didn't know anything about this until yesterday when some lunatic followed me around York. Before everything happened, I had

a good life with a great Mum and things were just... well, just fine! I didn't ask for any of this and I don't see how Tom keeps getting away with it. He followed a minor literally yesterday; can't you take him in for that?"

"He is currently under police custody," PC Blake says, speaking for what I think is the first time. She's always so quiet, watching as her partner leads the questioning. But he looks furious with her, his eyes warning her to keep quiet. But it's too late; I'm invested now.

"What do you mean?"

PC Blake takes a glance at the other officer before deciding to do what she thinks is right.

"He was caught on CCTV last night," she begins. "At the amusements down by the beach. He staged an attack."

Shit. Shit. Shit.

They know. They *have* to know.

There is no way that they looked at the footage and didn't see who he was hurling his weapons at. And that's why PC Clarke has been so suspicious about my answers; he thinks I'm hiding something but not what I thought he was getting at... None of this is about the diary! It's about the fact I was attacked by Tom last night and I didn't say a single thing to anyone. Do they think I'm trying to protect him or something? Do they think I was involved in my Mum's death?

"From last night's events alone, we have been able to detain him in a cell," PC Clarke reluctantly explains. "He will most likely receive a sentence for threatening to kill."

"Who was he trying to kill?" Steve says as I tense beside him.

I try to remain as calm as possible but once PC Clarke looks directly at me, my cover is blown.

Twenty Seven

"It was me," I admit, almost scared to look at my Uncle. But I do; I brave it, watching his brows furrow. "We didn't mean to do anything. We were just - "

"*We?*" Steve repeats. "Who else were you with?"

"Brodie and Zoe," I tell him. I can't exactly hide it now, can I? Besides, I'd rather they all know about the diner than the diary, if I have to choose between them.

"What were you all doing? You were grounded! *Are* grounded, I should say." He seems so annoyed at me but not in the way I expected; there's that same look of pity as he avoids my eye contact, the one that makes me feel like the victim in a sob story.

I suppose that's what I am now. I'm the daughter left behind.

All because of a car accident and a secret from the past.

All of it has brought me to the police station today, talking to officers about the man who murdered my Mum.

It's crazy, right?

Why don't I get to be one of those normal teenagers? My only concerns would be inward; I'd worry about how I look... about fitting in... about boys. Because I think about those things too from time to time; they're just clouded by this bigger thing. This pain in my chest that will probably never heal.

It's unfair. That's all it is.

And I'm tired of it.

"Gracie, we still have some more questions for you," PC Clarke says, reminding me of where I am as if I could forget.

I look up at him, barely processing his words.

"Why did you go out last night after what happened in York? Did you not feel unsafe?"

"I'm a teenager," I say. Surely that's a good enough excuse? I'm sixteen; hanging out with my friends at the amusements is a normal thing to do. In fact, it's the most mundane thing that I've done in a long time.

"Well, yes, but you were followed by a strange man yesterday," he continues. "Wouldn't you be scared to be out of your home?"

"It's not my home," I reply. "My home is in Green Haven."

"Answer the question, Gracie," PC Clarke says, refusing to follow my tangent.

"I didn't think he would try anything if I was with other people," I reply.

"But you weren't alone when you were in York when he followed you, were you?"

Shit.

"Were you?" he repeats again.

"No."

"So, I ask you again: wouldn't you be scared to be out of your home?"

He isn't going to leave it alone. He clearly thinks he's onto something, found a snag to grab a hold of and try and figure all of this out. But why am I being labelled guilty? Out of all the people in this room, I am quite literally the most innocent. All three of them have been lying to me all year long about my own Mum. I smoked a few cigarettes and went out with my friends. Lock me up, then, for doing absolutely fuck all.

"I wanted to hang out with my friends and there was no way that Steve or Debbie were going to let Zoe come over," I say casually. There, try that on for size. "A lot happened yesterday; I wanted to talk to my best friend about it, is that a problem?"

"But were you *scared*?"

"Did you want me to be or something?" I throw back at him. "This is a small town compared to York; everyone knows everyone and nothing ever happens."

"But still," he carries on. "You can see why we would be curious."

"Maybe," I play along. "But, at the end of the day, I'm a sixteen year old girl who has just found out her Mum was murdered. Can you not just let me process it in my own way?"

"We would love to," PC Blake steps in. "But this is really important; we need to help find justice for your Mum."

"So why are you treating me like I'm a suspect?" I say, calling them out bluntly. I'm fed up of dancing around it all, playing their little game of 'catch the murderer'.

"Because you are," PC Clarke says. His partner whips her head to him, looking just as confused as me.

"What?" I falter. I look to Steve for some kind of support, answers, I don't know. He looks just as dumbfounded as me.

"You were close to her and you have no alibi," PC Clarke explains monotonously. "You have lied multiple times during this interview. You even lie to your Aunt and Uncle."

"Hold on now, that's just what kids do," Steve interrupts.

"With all due respect, she's sixteen," he adds.

"Meaning, legally, she is still a child," Steve argues. "That's it; this interview is over. It's clearly not going to be helpful. Come on, Gracie."

I hesitate on the sofa, unsure if we're actually even allowed to just leave like this. But I'm not going to stay here by myself. If it was just PC Blake giving the interview, I wouldn't mind staying; she seems to actually care, unlike the other officer who has no kind bone in his body. But PC Clarke is strange; there is something dark about him. Something wrong. And so I follow after Steve, avoiding the confused looks of the police and closing the door after me.

"What do we do?" I say to him, feeling as young as I am for the first time in ages. I hate it.

"Uhm, I'm not too sure," he says. "I didn't really think past leaving. Maybe I should call Debbie."

"Isn't she at work?" I question.

"Yes but I think she will want to know how it went," he says. "Can you go and wait in the car and I'll be down shortly?"

He passes me the keys and I take them with a small nod. I'll happily leave the station; it gives me the jitters.

But as soon as the street air hits my face, I think about PC Clarke's words: *But were you scared?*

Was I? I guess so but I really did think that everything would be okay with Brodie and Zoe there. I suppose I really underestimated Tom too; stalking me around a city is one thing, throwing sports equipment to try and hurt me is a completely different thing, one that I don't understand.

I unlock the car and climb into the passenger seat, locking myself in (and other people out). Maybe I should have been more careful recently but then again, maybe they should have just been honest about what's going on. None of them care about how I feel…

I spent a year trying to come to terms with my Mum's death and now I feel like I'm going to have to start all over again. She didn't just *die*. She was *killed*. Cut away from this world by a terrifying man with a secret motive. Part of me wants to talk to Tom, to ask him *why*. Why kill her? Why follow me? Why attack me and my friends? There are too many 'why's.

But would he tell me anything? Probably not.

Steve's key is sharp on my skin as I trail the metal end against the side of my hand. I need to feel something different, something that isn't the pain I've been feeling all year. Now would be a great time to haul myself away somewhere with a cigarette, to feel the smoke against my face and forget about everything. But I don't have any left. I used my last one from the pack at the memorial and I've been too distracted to bother with them since. But things have changed now. Things are *worse*.

Brodie might hook me up with some more if I ask. Or he might be too worried about me now, too concerned with my safety to indulge me.

Ugh, forget it. All I really want to do right now is read my Mum's dairy and find out what happened next. With only three months left of the pregnancy, Tom had been threatening to kill her so that she couldn't have me; he clearly didn't succeed because I'm here now. But maybe he's spent all this time trying to finish what he started? He got rid of her but now he wants me gone too: everything about that time of his life vanishing with our last breaths.

As I stare down the street at the pavement, I almost wait for him to emerge from around the corner, walking directly towards me with a knife. His eyes would pierce mine as I held tight to the door handle, terrified that he would be able to prise it open. But why bother with a door when you can smash the window?

No matter how much I'm scared of it happening, I know that it can't. I don't trust PC Clarke but he wouldn't lie about Tom being in a cell because of last night's event. For now, I'm safe.

But am I in the long run? With every day that passes, I feel closer and closer to an end. Whether or not it's a good one, I'm unsure.

Twenty Eight

Once we get home again, Steve says that I can hang out at home and do anything I want, as long as I don't leave. I don't really understand why since Tom is currently behind bars and this is the safest I've technically been my whole life but then again, I am grounded. I really shouldn't be. But what am I supposed to do? Argue and have it extended? No thanks.

I go straight up to my room and find the bag with Mum's diary in, hauling it over my shoulder and knocking on Brodie's door.

"You back, then?" he says, swinging it open softly. His hair is marked from headphones; I've clearly interrupted a gaming session.

"Yeah," I reply. "Do you want to read the diary with me? I can message Zoe too, maybe."

"Definitely," he says, a little more excitably than I expected. "Give me two minutes and I'll meet you in the loft?"

"Yep," I say, heading up there straight away and firing off a message to Zoe. It feels right to have her here for it, to be just as involved. She's been so supportive and lovely; the first friend I've made since it happened. She replies almost instantly and I can't be surprised like I once would have been.

> Of course I'll be there! I'll set off in 5 and have my dad give me a lift.

And then a moment later:

> Don't worry, I'll have him drop me around the corner xx

> Thank you!

> See u soon xx

I'm so relieved that she can come and be here with me. It's all freaking me out, even more so than before, and I just need everything to be calm. That's it. Quiet. Still.

"How was the police station?" Brodie asks, reminding me of one of the main things I'm trying so hard to forget about. He takes a seat on the sofa next to me, ruffling his hair in a nonchalant fashion.

"Terrible," I say, refusing to sugar-coat it. "They think that I'm guilty!"

"What the fuck?" he questions.

"Exactly!" I say back, glad that he agrees. "They're literally rubbish at their job; it's no wonder they haven't been able to arrest him for her murder. It's like they don't want it to be him."

"Maybe they're just cautious," he argues.

"Oh yeah and that's why they've doubled down heavy on me being a part of it. Why the fuck would I kill my own Mum? How twisted is that?"

"Maybe they don't think you *killed* her, as such," he suggests. "Just that you and Tom are in cahoots or something."

"As if I'd do that," I complain, rolling my eyes. "The man is a psychopath. That's it."

"I can agree with you there," Brodie nods. "Do you think your Mum's diary will have more about it all? Maybe answer a few things?"

"I hope so."

"Why did you change your mind about handing it in?" he asks.

I'm surprised he has waited this long to bring it up, to be fair.

"Is it stupid to say that I feel like it's the only way to be close to her?" I admit. I hate this whole 'vulnerability' thing. It makes me feel weak, stupid… useless.

"Not at all," he says. "Actually, I think it's the most honest you've ever been with me."

"I'm sorry," I say. It's long overdue; I have been a bit of a bitch a few times.

"Don't sweat it, Gracie," he replies. "I probably would have been just as closed off as you in the situation."

"Even though your Mum's a witch?" I say but I regret it straight away. "Okay, okay, too much. Sorry."

"She's not perfect; she just cares," he adds. "She's really worried about you. We all are, I know it's gross."

"Yes, very gross. Let's stop now," I say. Then my phone buzzes. "Zoe is here. I'm gonna let her in through the window."

"Why don't you just tell her to knock?"

"Because I'm grounded?" I remind him.

"If Steve says no, I'll tell him you've had a tough day and it's a good thing that you're going to someone for support."

"Ugh, fine," I say. "Let me tell her."

> u can knock. Brodie has a plan to get u in so u don't have to climb.

> Should I be worried? Haha

> I'm always worried when it comes to Brodie's ideas.

But a moment later, we hear her knocking. I follow Brodie down the stairs, back to the upstairs landing, but he holds out a hand.

"I'll say I invited her over for you," he whispers.

I nod, thinking it's a decently good plan. I tuck myself away behind the banister, listening out for voices and the door. It swings open.

"Hello?" It's Steve's voice, confused but calm.

"Hi, uhm, I'm here to see Gracie," she says.

I actually kind of feel a little bad for Zoe right now because we didn't exactly fill her in on what she's meant to be doing and saying. But, then again, I don't have a clue either.

"It was me," Brodie says, reaching the bottom of the stairs. "Gracie is struggling a bit at the moment, you know, with all the stuff about her Mum. I thought she could do to have some support from the one friend that she's made."

Ouch.

"Oh, I mean, maybe we should ask your Mum," Steve stutters, clearly worried about what Debbie will think of it all. But she's not here. "Well, I guess it's alright as long as you stay in the house."

"Thanks, Dad," Brodie says. "Come in, Zoe. Gracie is upstairs."

I'm in utter shock that it worked but I'm just relieved when I meet them at the top of the stairs. Brodie points with his head that we should go back up to the attic; it's much more private there. Besides, I left the diary on the sofa. We head up, Zoe and I curling up close to each other and Brodie sitting in his usual corner of the sofa.

"So, you want the update?" I say to Zoe. I can't believe what I'm about to say but it's kind of important information in all of this mess. "The police think I'm involved."

"What the actual fuck?" Zoe questions, having a similar reaction.

"It's so stupid." Brodie shakes his head.

"They know I'm lying about something," I continue. "But they don't know it's about the diary."

"So, they think that must mean you killed your own Mum?"

"Not exactly," I answer. "But that I am helping Tom to cover his tracks."

"To be fair to them," Brodie cuts in. "It is weird how they haven't been able to find any evidence. You'd think the police would be able to solve it easily."

"So why can't they?" I say.

"You don't think they're purposefully trying to let him off lightly?" Zoe suggests.

It seems odd to even be an idea but she's got a point; PC Clarke has been far from professional with me, always stamping down on me and trying to catch me out. He's clearly not good at looking in the right places for his evidence if he's coming to me. But that doesn't mean he's in on it too; after all, he seems to *want* Tom to go down for this.

"Do you think it's all because they don't have the car?" I ask.

"I can't believe that a car could just vanish," Brodie says. "There would be things to track it... CCTV... tyre marks on your..." He freezes, realising that perhaps he shouldn't say what he was going to.

"On her body, I know," I finish for him. "I think that they were so concerned with getting her to the hospital once they realised she was still alive. She died in those clothes... they have to have kept them and tested them. But surely that would tell them what kind of car it was? Tom's family has a garage; wouldn't it be easy to trace it back to them?"

"Or easier for them to cover it up," Brodie shrugs. "Think about it; if this was a planned thing, Tom could have easily changed his tyres beforehand. He knows these things, even if he isn't an officer."

"But every time I've been around Tom," I begin. "He's not seemed completely there in his head, like maybe he's not okay mentally. I can't see him being smart enough to cover his tracks, especially with how open he's been with it all recently. It's like he wants to be caught."

"That makes no sense," Zoe says. "Why would you want to go to prison for murder?"

"I don't know... I don't understand any of this."

"Maybe the diary will help," Zoe reminds me.

I've been holding it on my lap, simply feeling it against my legs and being scared to open it.

"Yeah, I hope so," I whisper. I turn softly to the next entry and take a deep breath.

2nd January 2002

Dear Diary,

As of yet, Tom hasn't been able to follow through on his promise to kill me, thank God. It's not like he hasn't tried, though.

His family were over at ours for Christmas dinner (who's terrible idea was that?!?!) and he tried to burn my arm with the kettle when he was making the gravy. No one else was in the kitchen to see and who would believe me? So I told no one and instead ran my arm under the cold tap for a few minutes, hoping it wouldn't leave too big of a scar. There is a bit of a mark but the burns weren't too severe since I got to them pretty quickly.

He didn't seem happy about that. He was practically glaring at me through the entire dinner, only sporting a smile when someone spoke to him. How do they not see the evil in his eyes? How didn't I?

I'll never forgive myself for getting with him. For going along with it all despite the fact that it absolutely terrified me and didn't feel right. But I wouldn't take it back because then I wouldn't have my little girl…

I can't wait to meet her, to love her in the way that I never am. As soon as she's born, I'm taking her away from this town. We will get our own place… I'll get a job, anything. And I will never see Tom again.

I want to keep her safe. It's all I want.

Eve

Twenty Nine

She really did love me, I knew it then and I know it more now. Everything that Eve did after she became pregnant with me was to put me first; she even uprooted her life here and moved to Green Haven to get me away from him. I suddenly feel guilty for always wanting to ask her about my Dad; she kept quiet because it really was better not to know. But still, I wish I could have thanked her, let her know that I appreciated her. Those words are harder to say when someone is alive, though. And then... it's too late. One day, they are no longer here and you can't do anything about it other than scream at the world.

"It was very beautiful," Zoe says kindly.

"But not very helpful," Brodie adds. "Read the next one. We don't have long with the police on our backs now."

I nod and wipe away a small tear from my cheek. He's right; we don't have certainty about anything now. We have to keep on moving forward, trying to piece everything together by ourselves. Try to remember her properly and truthfully.

But when I read the date for the next entry, anxiety bubbles in my stomach. For the first time, I'm no longer in her womb... I was born only a week before she wrote this.

18th March 2002

Dear Diary,

I left the hospital a few days ago, signing myself out now that I'm eighteen. I didn't tell anyone; I simply caught a bus and headed to the town I picked out a while ago: Green Haven. It's a small place, one based on community, and I think it will be good for us.

And by us... I mean Gracie. That's what I've decided to name her. I think it's fitting.

I don't have much to give her but I have my allowance saved up and some money from Christmas. I knew that I'd be needing it so I've kept every morsel that I can. Tom also has to pay child support so I'll get that into my bank every month, not that it will be a lot. He doesn't give two hoots about her so luckily I doubt he will be arguing over custody. At least that's one thing I don't need to worry about.

I've only got a couple hundred pounds... enough to cover a room at the singular hotel here for a few nights and food. I've been breastfeeding Gracie; I know that it's best for her. I'll always want to do right by her; I just hope that I'll be able to.

After a few days here, I was beginning to worry about how I was going to get money... how I was going to raise a child by myself with no house... no job, only the child support money coming in once a month, barely making a dent.

But then I saw a little hand-written sign in a window. It was the florist. I had Gracie with me but I went in all the same, holding her close to me. The woman at the counter seemed kind enough so I asked about the job. She said it was only miniMum wage, a few shifts a week. But I said I'd take it if she'd let me have it.

She was desperate, bless her, and said that now she was getting older, things were becoming harder for her.

And so when I mentioned about having to find someone to watch Gracie, she said that she could *stay at the shop with me! And get this! She has a spare room!*

Sheila is so lovely. I don't know what I would have done if she hadn't have let me stay in her little flat above the shop. I'm going to work as hard as I can to prove to her that she wasn't wrong to give me a chance. I think it will do Gracie good to have a role model too.

Overall, I think we will be okay.

My parents are furious but I'm eighteen now. They know they don't have a say anymore and I can't bring Gracie up in that house, especially with Tom so close by. If he ever sees her, I'll never forgive myself. There's something wrong with him... something terrible.

Eve

This entry was tough to read; not that the others weren't but this one is different. I exist in this part of the timeline. I'm a part of the story.

"So that explains a lot," I sigh. "No wonder she never said about growing up here. It sounds like she was terrified. Imagine how she'd feel is she knew I live here now, only a few streets away from him. It was the one thing she was trying to avoid."

"It's not your fault, though," Zoe says. "I'm sure she could have never predicated this."

"But she did!" I cry. "She's said multiple times in these entries that he wants to kill her and her answer is to run away because she didn't think anyone would believe her over him. It's so fucked up."

"So let's figure it out," Zoe says. "You don't trust PC Clarke, right?"

I shake my head.

"Okay, so how about we go down to the station and ask to speak to just PC Blake? Say that you didn't feel comfortable with him there and it was making it harder. And then… maybe… you can give her the diary."

"She did seem like she really wanted to help," I admit. "PC Clarke just wants to arrest me for some deluded reason."

"Yeah, so forget about him," Zoe continues. "We can even report him. I'm sure there's a thing about officers acting a certain way; you could maybe have him removed from the case completely."

"Do you think?" I ask, my eyes widening. The idea seems amazing.

"Why not? He's clearly not being objective," Zoe says. "Come on, what do you say? This is for your Mum, remember. It's all for her."

"I just don't know if I can go back there…" I say. The thought of walking back through the front doors of the police station is truly terrifying. I don't know if I can do it. But then again, my Mum did things she didn't think she could do just so that I would be safe... Surely I owe her this?

"Brodie and I will go with you if that will help?" she suggests.

"Maybe..." I say. "Can we read another entry, though? If I have to hand it over, I want to read as much as I can first."

"Of course," she replies softly.

And, like it's become a habit, I turn the page over and begin the next entry, bracing my breath.

22nd June 2002

Dear Diary,

Sorry I haven't written! Life has been hectic. I'm still at the florist shop, living with Sheila in her spare room. But I'm beginning to save up a bit of money which is amazing! She only charges me a tiny bit of rent each week so she can cover the extra bills I'm using but it's so little that it barely makes a difference.

I even got a second job on the days that the shop is closed. Sheila watches Gracie for me while I'm there. It's at a little cafe and it's only down the *road from the florist so it's super easy for getting back and forth!*

I was a little nervous to leave Gracie at first but Sheila is so good to her. She's almost like a grandma! I think she probably fancies herself as that, if I'm honest. But I love it so much, seeing Gracie all spoiled and loved. It makes me feel like I made the right decision in coming here. I just hope that we can stay like this: happy.

Eve

It genuinely seems like we were happy in Green Haven, even though it followed on from the most awful events. Come to think of it, I don't think I was ever *un*happy at any point before last year; our life was perfect. Until it wasn't. Because she no longer had hers.

"I wonder why Tom didn't bother her at first," Zoe questions, waking me from my thoughts. "He'd always said to your Mum that he didn't want anything to do with you. Wouldn't he have just been happy that she'd upped and left him and the town all together? Why come back fifteen years later?"

"I don't know," I admit. She's got a great point; something isn't adding up.

"Sorry to be the one to ask," Brodie says. "But are we certain it was Tom who killed her?"

"Why would you even say that?" I ask, a little bit of annoyance at the back of my throat. It's so deadly obvious that it was him; he practically admitted in the record store. Oh my God. The record. I'd stashed it in my room and forgotten all about it in the mess of everything. At least that is one small comfort I have. I can just imagine sitting down to listen to it... I just need a record player first. The one that my Mum bought us from a charity shop is long gone, sold along with most of her other things to pay for the funeral.

"Well," Brodie continues. "The police are struggling to find evidence against him. It's like they keep wandering down the wrong paths, like blaming you to try and explain why they can't pin it on Tom."

"But he came up to me," I remind him. "He said that she deserved it."

"Yeah but that isn't him admitting it," he says. "Maybe he was happy about the fact she died. Sorry, that sounds really harsh, but it's not like he liked either of you. He might have just known about the accident."

"So, why follow me?"

"Maybe seeing Eve's death brought some things up for him?" Zoe adds.

"You're not believing this theory too?" I question her. She's always been on my side, supporting me even when I didn't think I was worth it.

"We should at least consider it," Zoe argues softly. She looks almost scared to be going against me but it's not like I'm going to do anything. I'm not Tom. "This is all to bring justice for your Mum, right? Maybe there is a reason the police haven't found any answers after a year."

I've only started to process that my Mum's death wasn't an accident. Yet, now I might have to accept that Tom isn't even the one who murdered her.

I just want to know.

No.

I *need* to know. This pain is too much.

Thirty

Brodie's idea makes sense, I'll admit, I just don't want it to. Somehow not knowing what happened to her is worse than it being Tom's stupid fault; his wacked attempt at revenge, or something. But I've spent a whole year wondering who that driver was, who's car hit her, who could leave a dying woman alone in the street, not a care in the world if she survived or not.

So, honestly, I don't know how to react to it.

"Maybe we should tell the police this," Zoe says.

"Oh yeah, so it will look like I'm trying to point them away from me," I grunt. How on earth is it fair that telling the truth would make me look guilty of a crime that I didn't even commit in the first place?

"And they probably do have other suspects," Brodie sensibly adds. "They're not going to tell you everything; in fact, I reckon they aren't allowed to."

"But they should make an exception for me," I reply angrily. "I'm her daughter! I have nothing because of that idiot. Nothing."

"You have us," Zoe says, holding onto my arm.

I want it to be enough so bad but it's just not. Having Brodie and Zoe's support is one thing; what I really want, though, is my Mum to still be alive. I want to live in Green Haven, in the house that she spent years saving for, eating Sheila's brownies that she left the recipe for after she passed. I want to be blushing over that one random guy in my class who I didn't even like that much but has nice hair so why not.

I don't want any of this.

"So, what the fuck do we do?" I ask. But no one can answer because what *do* you do in these situations?

"I don't have a clue," Zoe says. "But I think we should do the right thing and go back to the station. You can tell them that you're not going to speak to anyone unless it's PC Blake. Won't that make it easier?"

"Maybe," I sigh. I hate the idea of going back; I literally embarrassed myself when I had a bloody panic attack in the staircase but also I hate that stupid officer. Why the fuck would *I* be a suspect? It makes no sense at all and I can't even piece together how he's come to that conclusion.

"Come on," she says. "Bring the diary; tell her that you want to keep it if you can. I don't know if they will let you but it's worth a try."

"And say you haven't read it yet but you weren't sure if it would help," Brodie adds. "They are the ones who told you about Tom so you can just say you didn't know if it would help but it might mention him."

"Good idea," Zoe says, nodding along. "See, it's all going to be fine."

But is it? Because all I can feel is vomit at the back of my throat.

...

Stepping back into the reception of the police station is no welcoming sight but what Zoe said before is true: this is the right thing to do for my Mum. The diary is tucked away in my bag. I can feel it against me, a reminder about everything.

"Ready?" Zoe whispers to me.

It feels like I've got a whole gang around me. There's Zoe beside me and then Steve and Brodie in front, my Uncle heading straight to the reception to ask if I could speak to PC Blake. I think he was a little shocked that I wanted to go back after what happened but at the end of the day, this is nothing compared to what my Mum had to endure.

"According to the system," the receptionist begins, focusing on the computer screen. "There are two officers assigned to the case, PC Clarke being the main one."

"I understand that," Steve says.

For a moment, I hold my breath, wondering if he is going to still stand by me.

"But my niece doesn't feel comfortable around him. She would much prefer to be alone with his partner."

"I'll see what I can do," is the answer.

"See, it'll be okay," Zoe whispers to me.

I wish I could believe her.

The receptionist heads through a door behind her desk, disappearing like she was never here to begin with. This whole thing makes me feel sick to my stomach and I still don't even feel certain that I should be here. It's all so damn confusing and I hate it. Have I said that? Maybe, but I don't think anyone will ever be able to understand what this feels like. It's the worst kind of pain I've ever had to go through.

She returns a moment later with a smile.

"They've agreed that it's okay," she says. "Would you mind going to the same interview room you were in earlier?"

Yes, yes I do mind.

"No problem," Steve says.

We follow after him through the door that the receptionist buzzes us through. I'm going have to go through it all over again. Why did I agree to this?

For her.

I need to remember that this is all for her. For justice. For everyone to remember her properly. It's like a mantra in my head; I've had to tell it to myself a million times at this point just to keep from completely losing it. And, even then, I could just curl up and cry right now. I'm not really the kind of person to cry over things but I think this is a valid exception.

Back then, when she was in the hospital, I cried so much. I didn't care that I looked stupid in front of the staff or that my Mum would be disappointed in me. All that mattered was that she was wasting away right in front of me, drifting closer to death with every moment that her body was attached to those tubes.

But after she was gone, I couldn't bring myself to allow it. I was around new people now, people who I had barely spent any time with. I didn't want to look weak to them, to look like the kind of girl who would completely break down because of one small moment. Mum always taught me to be strong but she also said it was important to be myself; how do I do both?

I climb the stairs almost robotically, trying not to think too much about earlier. I'm relieved as fuck when we reach our floor but it's short lived when we stand outside the door to the interview room. PC Blake is already there waiting for us, clearly having been notified by the receptionist. She looks a little nervous; that makes two of us.

"Thanks for coming back, Gracie," she says softly. "I know how difficult all of this is for you."

I genuinely believe every word that she is saying; the moment confirms that I can trust her. Whether or not I'm going to hand over the last connection to my Mum is a different story all together, though. I'd be signing away the closest thing I have to being able to talk to her and that's a tough decision to make.

"Why don't we all go in," PC Blake says. "You're friends can come in too if that would help?"

"Yes, please," I say, thankful that she already seems way better than her partner. PC Clarke is a prick.

"Come on, then," she smiles, opening the door.

We all trail in, taking whatever empty seat we can find on the sofas. Zoe sits directly beside me, refusing to leave my side and I love her for it.

"As we did earlier, I will have to record this interview," PC Blake says. "I hope that's okay?"

"I understand," I say. I'm not entirely okay with it because it means that her piss take of a partner is going to hear it. To be fair, he's probably listening in right now to our every word; why else would they have been okay to let the lead officer on the case sit out?

She clicks the recording on and does the same introduction she had done earlier.

Breathe, Gracie. Just breathe.

"So, how come you changed your mind?" is the first question. Her voice wobbles a bit as though she hasn't led an interview before. Honestly, she probably never gets a chance to get a word in if she has to work with PC Clarke all the time.

"I want to help as much as I can," I begin. "I just really struggled with how PC Clarke was speaking to me. It made me very uncomfortable when I was already super nervous." I really hope that he's listening now so that I can turn the table and make him question his behaviour. He's a grown man bullying a sixteen year old; he needs to grow the fuck up. I can't believe I let him upset me.

"I see," she replies, looking a bit uncomfortable herself. But there's something in her eyes that makes me think she agrees with me. "So, would you be able to tell me your thoughts on everything?"

"What do you mean?" I ask.

"I guess, if you could go through who you think did it, what you think about Tom, those kinds of things?"

"Right," I say. "Uhm. Well, I think Tom has some weird justification to do something like that if he really wanted to. I'm not excusing him but I do think that he might have done it."

"Okay, that's good, well, not good but you know, good for the case," she stumbles.

"Yeah," I reply. "I don't know if it's him one hundred percent, though," I add, remembering what the three of us had been speaking about in the loft only an hour ago.

"Oh?"

"I've been thinking about what Tom said to me," I explain. "At the record store in York. He never admitted to it, he just said he deserved it. And what if you guys haven't been able to find any evidence against him because it wasn't actually him?"

I wait for her to reply but no words come from her mouth. Instead, she's blinking at me, shocked that I've even mentioned it as an option.

"Sure, he has a reason why he would want her dead but that doesn't mean he went and did it," I continue. "You guys would have been able to prove it ages ago. You can track phones and analyse tyres and things like that. Why are you so desperate to see Tom go down?"

"Well, uhm," the officer says. "He seemed the most likely suspect. The truth is, we don't have any other suspects."

"So you wanted any evidence at all to stick the blame on an innocent?" Steve questions. Gosh, I don't think I've ever seen him so angry before and I've pissed him off loads in the past year.

"It's not like that," PC Blake says. "He is definitely our most likely suspect but we have a few other ideas that we are wanting to follow up. We just don't have the funds to do that yet."

Are they kidding?

"My mother's death hasn't been brought to justice because of money?"

"In a roundabout way, yes," she admits. "The town is so small that even working with Green Haven's police, we don't have as many resources as a city would. It makes it a lot harder to cover all of our tracks quickly."

"I can't believe this," Steve mutters.

"It's why it's so important that we get as much help from you as possible," she continues. "If it was up to me, I would have done so much more but I'm a rookie on the job. I'd barely started my first shift last year. But I can help you now, if you'll let me."

This is it. My turning point.

Do I tell her about the diary; more importantly, do I *really* trust that she can help?

Thirty One

It's a tough decision, that's plain and simple. But there's so much riding on it. It could quite literally change the direction of the entire case, pointing them down another path or perhaps straight back to Tom. It could still be him, though, and I don't want to write that off. Honestly, I'd love to see him behind bars. At least he will probably spend some time in prison for the events at the diner, even if it is far from long enough.

"I do have one question," I ask. "If it wasn't Tom, why did he try to attack me last night?"

"Well, that's what we have to consider," PC Blake answers. "It's another sign that makes him *seem* guilty while also not *proving* he was driving the car that killed her. I'm not sure if I should even be telling you this but we've got it confirmed that Tom's phone wasn't anywhere near the accident site."

"What does that mean?"

"It means that he either has a genius alibi or that he wasn't responsible," she says. "We can't confirm either way. There also weren't any tyre marks on her clothes or body; he most likely hit her head on."

My stomach crunches at the imagery.

"I know it's awful to hear, I'm really sorry," she says. "But I think it's more useful for you to know the details, even if others disagree."

I can almost sense the presence of PC Clarke outside of the room, listening in on her words and I smile.

"It makes it really difficult to identify what kind of car hit her," she continues. "There isn't even any CCTV in the area; the cons of living in such a small and safe town. Green Haven really lives up to its name."

Not enough, I think.

"While we can't prove where Tom was that night," she carries on. "We do have reason to believe that he might have acted violently towards Eve, like he did with you last night. But it feels like we're missing a piece of the puzzle, holding us back from the confirmation we need."

"Okay," Steve says, clearly having been thinking quite hard about all of this. "He didn't have his phone on him, right? How can we go about finding out if he was responsible? What would we need?"

"Anything that relates to Tom in any way will be helpful, no matter what it is," she answers. "Even the most mundane things can give us clues. We're going around in circles at the moment, stuck looking at the same few leads until we're right back at square one. Other than Tom's connection to Eve when they were teens, we've got nothing to suggest that they were in contact after that. It would be strange for him to come back and seek revenge - or whatever he was trying to do - over a decade later."

They need the damn diary.

I exchange a subtle glance with Brodie; he's thinking the same thing. And I don't dare look at Zoe since she's right beside me but I know what she would say.

"I might have something."

Am I really doing this?

Fuck. Fuck. Fuck.

I hate it. I hate it so fucking much. But Mum, this is all for you. It's always for you.

"I have my Mum's diary."

...

As soon as I've said the words, I can't take them back. It's all so sickening; my worry is encased in an anxiety that I'll lose my Mum all over again. I might have to walk out of this police station without it, even though it's been my entire life for a while now, something to hold onto and look forward to.

"Do you have it with you?" PC Blake asks. She seems excited at the thought, as though it really will make a difference, and that makes me feel a little better about the situation.

"Yes," I whisper. I tug my bag closer to me, tracing the straps. She isn't going to rush me; it's clear in the way that she holds herself that she cares about my wellbeing in all of this. I can take my time, thinking about everything far too much. Opening up the bag, I reach in slowly, feeling the edges of the notebook like I've done so many times before. But now is different; there's always been a risk involved but never one with the chance of losing it completely. But as I slide it out, I feel everyone's eyes on me; I can't change my mind now. "It's here."

"May I?" PC Blake asks kindly, gesturing to the diary.

I take another look at it, trying not to cry. It might just be a stupid book from long ago but it's so much more than that to me. But I hand it out to her, watching as it passes from my hand to hers.

"Thank you, Gracie," she replies. She's holding it so carefully, almost as though it's priceless. "Have you read any of it?"

"Bits and pieces," I admit. "I wasn't sure if it would be helpful but it does mention Tom in there."

"Where did you find this?" Steve asks, reminding me that I wasn't even supposed to have it in the first place.

"It was me," Brodie says. "I thought she should have it. It was her Mum's, after all."

"Right," Steve replies. It's not like he can do anything here; there are bigger things going on.

"For the record, how long have you had this?" PC Blake asks.

"Uhm, since the memorial," I say, wracking my brain. "We've been reading it together, trying to feel connected to her."

So, you were withholding evidence?" the officer reluctantly asks, leaning back on the sofa.

I never even thought about it in that way. All I saw was something that belonged to my Mum, something that is mine by proxy.

"I just wanted a way of feeling close to her again, like she's still here," I tell her. "I don't even know if it's going to be helpful. I've not read all of it."

"Would we be able to keep this, to look through?" she asks.

"Can I have it back?"

"Eventually," she says truthfully. "I can't promise how long the team will need it. Someone will have to read through it and put it against our theories."

"But when you're finished with it, it's mine again?" I ask, practically begging for an answer.

"It's always *yours*, Gracie," she replies. "I'll make sure it's' taken good care of. In the meantime, is there anything you have read that you think is important to bring up now?"

I wrack my brain, thinking over all the words.

"Tom used to threaten my Mum when she was pregnant with me," I stutter. It was awful to read but even worse to say out loud in a police station. "She was too scared to tell anyone because she thought that they wouldn't believe her."

"That's not true," Steve sighs.

"What?" I say. What does he mean?

"It's not true," he repeats, combing his fingers though his hair. "She told Debbie."

"Debbie knew?" I gasp in horror. "She knew he was dangerous and she didn't do anything?" I can't believe it. I've never really like Debbie but it was only ever because she was super annoying. But this? This is different.

"Eve told her everything shortly after she moved to Green Haven," Steve explains. He's struggling through the words; it must have been a difficult time for everyone, not just my Mum. "She was finding it hard at first, feeling isolated. She'd never been close to her parents but Debbie and her used to be when they were younger. She might have written about it in the diary; it would have been January 2003, Gracie's first birthday."

"Can we read it?" I ask PC Blake desperately.

"Yes, of course," she says. She begins to flick through the notebook. Even though she is turning the pages carefully, I still wish it could be me. But then again, my voice is already wobbly enough; I'd never be able to read it well enough for everyone to listen.

"I found it," PC Blake says. And then, she reads my Mum's words.

15th March 2003

Dear Diary,

I invited Debbie to come over for Gracie's first birthday... and she came. I was so nervous; I thought she'd use it as an opportunity to tell me off, to shout at me for running away. But she was strangely proud. She was so polite to Sheila, not judging any of us for the situation I'm in. In fact, she thought it was a really nice thing of Sheila to take us in, to make sure that we were safe. Apparently I'd really worried her when I'd left, my parents too.

So, why didn't they come after me?

Debbie says they didn't want to bother after a while, that they were too disappointed in me. She doesn't agree with them, though. She even brought Steve and little Brodie over to make sure I had family with me. It'll do Gracie some good too.

It was all going so well... they'd brought a cake and presents, celebrating my daughter's birthday as though the past two years never happened. So I decided to tell her some things.

Debbie and I went to a nearby cafe to talk privately. I told her all the things that Tom had threatened me with, all the things he promises to do to me when I was pregnant.

"No wonder you left," is all she said at first. It felt so good to have someone understand why I did it, why I had to go. And what's even better... she believed me. Every word. Every memory.

I asked about Tom then, knowing that he was still living only a few streets away. She didn't want to tell me at first, said it was better that I didn't know. But I begged and she relented.

He still goes over to my parents' house for dinner every Friday.

And he's still got everyone wrapped around his little finger, acting as the golden child like I had run away from, stealing his baby. But where were the child benefit payments from him? They'd stopped almost as quickly as they'd started and he didn't even ask to see her. I thought he wanted to pretend that it had never happened, so why is he spending his evenings at my family home, playing his messed up little role?

Debbie doesn't trust him; she thinks that something is going on. I don't know, though...he's just a teenage boy whose life I've wrecked by giving in to him. It hurts to think how naive I was when I first met him; I thought he was going to be my first real love... the first boy I ever gave my heart to. But I grew up because of him. I learned that *people can hurt you, even if I could never do it myself.*

Either way, whether he's up to something or not, I can't do anything except for carry on as I am, hoping that he will keep out of it.

Eve

It's really odd to think that Debbie and my Mum liked each other at one point. I don't have many memories of seeing my Aunt and Uncle while I was growing up, so who knows what happened there. But someone believed my Mum; someone listened to her and was there for her when I couldn't be. And that makes me feel really good.

Thirty Two

"That was very helpful," PC Blake says, reminding me that I'm here for more than just reliving memories.

"It certainly points us in the direction of Tom again, right?" Steve asks.

But before he can get an answer, the door swings open. It's PC Clarke. I freeze on the sofa, clenching my body and staring at him.

"We've had a few updates," he says, looking at his partner. "We need you to come and have a look."

"Right," PC Blake says, not really sure how to react. However, at the end of the day, she's practically a newbie here; she has to follow orders, do what she's told. "Gracie, do you mind if I take your Mum's diary?"

"I guess that's fine," I say. I need to be strong now; she said it will be helpful and I need to believe in that. It's the only thought that will get me through this.

"Thank you for trusting me," she replies and I nod, begging her to just go so I don't have to live in this moment any longer than I have to. She switches off the recording and heads out with PC Clarke, closing the door behind her.

I guess that means we aren't going anywhere just yet.

...

No one really knows what to say as we wait for her to return. I think they're all a little nervous to start a conversation because of how tense I seem; I wouldn't try either. The last time I felt like this was at my Mum's memorial; it was barely any time ago but it still feels like a lifetime ago. I was so angry at everyone for arriving in black and acting all depressed; back then, that was my biggest problem.

But now? Everything got so much worse, one step at a time, until the pain I used to feel became unrecognisable, small in contrast to the pure anger I feel at the world.

I never had any idea as to who was driving the car. It was labelled as an accident, some poor guilty person had hit her and driven away, tortured by what they had done. But learning about Tom changed everything; her death was no longer tragic. It was a murder. A brutality. And I don't think I'll ever move on until it's a case closed; the incident proved and the cell locked. I need that now, more than I ever thought I would. Because I don't think I can move on without the truth.

And so, when PC Blake returns, her eyes red and sore, I don't know what to think. It's like a thousand words are exchanged in our glance; the pain in our eyes calling out for the words that won't come easily.

"I have to speak to Gracie alone," she says gravely.

"Can't they stay with me?" I ask, scared for the first time in a year to be alone. I always thought that I would only ever want my Mum's company, unable to ever have it. Everyone else would feel second best in comparison, pointless and meaningless.

"If you would like," she nods. "I will need my Chief Constable to be here too, as per the policy."

I hate it. I hate it so much. But I can't throw a tantrum here now, not when there's something so significant that they need to tell me that it's made an officer cry. I have to be braver now than ever before; I need to make her proud.

"Okay."

"Thank you," she says. The door widens as she enters, followed by an older man in a slightly fancier version of the uniform I'm so used to seeing. You can tell he's in charge just by the way he carries himself; he's important and he knows it.

"Hello Gracie," he says. The two of them take a seat where PC Blake had been before.

Zoe wraps her hand in mine, realising what I need before I do.

"I have some news. I'm not sure how you are going to take it," the constable says. He looks reluctant to tell me but more able to than PC Blake. "As you know, we had Tom in one of our holding cells for what he did at the amusements. But we also sent him for questioning earlier today regarding your mother's case."

Is this where I find out? Is this the moment? After all this time?

"As expected, he wasn't too much help. He kept muttering things that didn't make sense."

"He was speaking in riddles," PC Blake adds.

"Yes," the constable continues, looking a little annoyed at her cutting in. "We had linguists watching the interview, as well as someone who is trained in analysing behaviour in criminals. We knew we weren't going to get much out of Tom's words alone."

"And what happened?" I dare to ask.

"He wasn't responsible for your mother's death."

What?

"I know it's probably not the news that you wanted," he continues.

But I'm barely listening. Why have they spent a whole year following the wrong person? Trying to convict the WRONG PERSON?

"How do you know?" I ask, my voice hoarse and desperate.

"Someone has come forward with some helpful information," he says, clearing his throat as though he hates admitting it. Of course he does; they've been looking in the wrong direction all year. "And it's proving to be a strong lead. But it would put Tom as innocent."

He's far from it.

"He was still going to be put on trial for the events at the diner," he explains. But hang on a second.

"Was?"

"Tom is no longer with us," he answers solemnly.

"As in?" I question; why can't they just be straight with us?

"He was found dead in his cell not long after he finished his interview."

Tom is dead.

My Dad is dead.

The man who didn't kill my Mum is dead.

"How?" Steve replies, brave enough to ask the question we all want to know the answer to.

The constable looks at him blandly, confused as to why it's even been brought up. I don't know why but it matters, it really does.

"Trauma to the head," he says calmly.

"But why? If he didn't kill her, why come after me? Why do that to himself?" I ask, begging to know more. I need to know more.

"We don't know for certain," he replies. "He wasn't very straight with us, never was really. I think he must have been troubled, though. He had a tough childhood from what we know."

So did my Mum but she didn't try to hurt anyone.

"I think it all just built up for him over the years," he goes on. "He wasn't sure how to cope with it all. And then, I guess he thought he was about to go down for something he didn't do; he got scared."

"He wasn't exactly a good man, though," I cut in. "He deserved to go to prison for what he did. He might not have killed my Mum but he tried to kill me!"

"Yes, I agree," he says. "But there's nothing we can do now, I'm afraid. All we can do is follow this new lead and try to figure out what happened that night. Anyway, I best be going. My condolences."

His *condolences*? What the actual fuck is wrong with him. Does he not care that someone meaningful and kind has died and that his officers have done nothing to help? But there's no point arguing. Within a moment, he's out in the hallway asking for a cup of tea.

"I'm sorry," PC Blake says. At least she looks it. "I know this isn't what you wanted to hear. The closure would have been good."

"Yeah," I agree. "What's this new lead, then? Who did it?"

"I'm not sure if I'm allowed to release that information yet," she admits. "As soon as I'm allowed, I promise I will tell you. But I will try and keep everyone on track a bit more than they have been; you went through something awful and they've handled it just as badly. I wish we could have done it differently back then and kept our options open; Tom just seemed like the man."

"Yeah," I say again. What else am I supposed to reply with? *Oh don't worry about it, it's okay! We all make mistakes!* Fuck that.

"You don't have to stay here any longer; you can go home if you'd like," she says. "And we won't be needing your Mum's diary anymore so I've asked for it to be sent to the reception for you."

I have to admit, I light up a little bit at this. The idea of still being able to talk to her in some way is somehow comforting in all of this, even if I didn't get the answers I want.

But as I hold it in my hands again, it feels different now. Physically, it hasn't changed. But I know that the man she was once so scared of didn't get the satisfaction of taking her life, even if he wanted it so badly that he would come after me too. I hope she finds it reassuring, wherever she is now. I know that I do.

...

We've all been in a weird state of silence since we got home. Debbie arrives back from work not long after we get there and she looks deathly confused at the array of depressed faces on her pristine sofas.

"What happened?" she asks.

I can't bring myself to explain, to relive it through my own words. I lean back in the chair, the tears brimming along the corners of my eyes as I turn away from her. She can't see me cry.

"We've had a few updates," Steve says, motioning her into the kitchen. She follows after him, closing the door behind them, their whispers barely audible through the wall. Not that I need to hear; I know exactly what he's telling her.

"How are you doing?" Zoe asks me.

"I don't know," I admit, trying to hold onto the last bit of strength I have left within me. "I really thought it was him."

"But there was always a chance it wasn't," she reminds me. "Besides, it could still be good news."

"*Good news*?" I repeat. "How can anything related to my Mum's death be *good news*?"

"I just mean that maybe it was an accident after all."

"But it's not like they gave themselves in," Brodie adds, rolling his eyes.

Ugh. I hate this so much; that's all I can think. Zoe is trying to be nice, to make things easier; of course it will be better if it was an accident rather than cold-blooded murder. But Brodie also has a point. The driver could have held their hands up and admitted to it. And whether or not they meant to crash into her, it doesn't matter; they've hidden away for over a year now.

Debbie and Steve return; she looks appropriately white in the face now.

"Are you alright?" she says to me before doing anything else.

"Sure," I reply. "Why not?"

"I'm so sorry this is all happening, Gracie," she says. "We really all did think it was him. He was always so angry."

Like me.

But then we all freeze. Because there's a sound from the hallway. A loud, blearing ring.

The phone.

Dear diary

In the end, it doesn't seem to matter who had driven the car. Eve Myers is dead and always will be, once a daughter and a mum, but now only a memory. She became that the night at the hospital, after I'd ran through the corridors to find her room, only to see her already half alive. Everything after that maybe isn't as important as I once thought.

I still remember being told about what happened to the driver and their fate was nearly as bad as my mum's. Someone had called the station, telling them that they had found a car in a lake a few towns over. It caught all the police off guard; those kinds of things don't happen often around here. Crime in general is low but they sent a team to uncover the vehicle pretty quickly. It wasn't confirmed straight away who it belonged to but it has 'suspicious' written all over it. Besides, the case was taken up by York's police station; they have a bigger budget over there and sent things in for analysis.

The body was given an identity within a matter of weeks.

And the tyres. They were a match.

Mum's body had been relatively untouched by them when it happened but the road had a few marks on, just enough to make out. Just enough to confirm that it was this car that had done the damage, that had taken her life. There was no arrest to be made. No justice.

But there is an answer, finally. It's an unexpected one, that's for sure, but it's there all the same, a final edition to her story.

I read the rest of the diary over the following weeks, finding only comfort in the pages as they became more positive over the years. She wrote less and less, leaving bigger gaps between the entries, because she was happy, distracted.

The only secret ended up being the pain that my biological father left behind. But that lived mostly in the past, save for his little freak out. They think the guilt got to him after all these years, building up inside him and driving him crazy. I still don't know what to think about it, really. I'll never love him like I should love a dad. And I'll also never forgive him for how he was with her. But I don't need to. He made his choices, not me.

I'm still living with Debbie and Steve, only it's not as bad as it used to be. Things are finally starting to look up now that I'm not so angry anymore. It wasn't some awful person that stole her life; it was someone who was really struggling with their own. It's not something I ever really want to accept happened but I have to, otherwise how else can I move on? I don't want to forget her... to just leave her behind. I'll always try and keep her memory alive in any way I can.

Got to go now, though. Zoe is here and we're going to do something really special.

Update you later,

gracie

Epilogue

"It's a beautiful place," Zoe says as we walk along the grass, a muddle of stones around us.

There are probably a few hundred people buried here, resting peacefully beneath our feet. Green Haven has always been a tiny place; the church and its cemetery reflecting it perfectly. But it's nice. Yeah, it's really nice.

"Where is your Mum's grave?" she asks softly.

I look to the direction I know it is in. I've never visited, not once since she died, terrified for it to feel final. But I think I'm ready now.

Debbie said it was at the back of the church, out towards the fence. There's a recent stone there; I can see it from here. It must be the one. We walk towards it, our feet stepping along the grass.

It's so strange. All of it. I thought that I couldn't move on until I had answers but maybe that was just an excuse because I was scared. Even now that I know who the driver was, I'm not feeling happy or accepting about any of it. Her death is still real; it didn't undo it.

And so, I've come to the realisation that my healing journey has only just begun.

Her grave is different to how I imagined it.

Really, it just looks like every other one here, save for the fact it looks relatively recent and because of the words etched into the front: *Eve Myers, beloved daughter, sister and Mum*. She's here with me now but in a different way to how it is when I'm reading her diary or listening to the record I bought. She would have loved it and I can just about imagine her sat there with me, dragging me from my seat to dance together.

There's no music here. Just the sound of birds and cars on the passing road.

"We should put the flowers in for her," I say, remembering that we had bought some purple hydrangeas to leave for her. "Do you think there's a tap to fill the tub?"

"It will be by the church, most likely down the side," Zoe answers.

I pass her the flowers and bend down, taking the little metal pot from its place in the stone.

As we walk towards the church, I don't really know how to feel. It's a lot, that's for sure. All of these months have gone by without her and I know that it won't be long until I'll be saying 'years' instead. But I think I'm becoming more okay with it all. Obviously, I'm not over the moon or anything but I'm beginning to accept that it's happened and process it.

The tap is rusting but after a stiff turn to the right, cold water pours out onto the ground, splashing at our shoes.

"You should have held the pot under!" Zoe laughs, squealing as she throws herself back.

"I didn't think," I reply back, holding it under the tap. The water is freezing against my fingers but I like it; it makes me feel alive. And God do I love being alive.

"Right, that will do," I say, turning the tap off. "Let's go back."

The second walk to the grave isn't as bad as the first. I've seen the stone now, seen the grass that buries her in the earth. All that's left are the things that I can do from here; I can leave flowers and sit by the stone talking to her. I can tell her all the things I want to, just like before. She might not be able to reply but I'll know she's listening.

"I'll wait over here," Zoe says, standing a few rows away. "You have some privacy with her and I'll wait here as long as you need."

"Thank you," I say, pausing to take in how lucky I am as she hands me the flowers.

Zoe won't be around much longer. Her Mum got a new job and they're having to move over the summer holidays. She will be at a new sixth form and make new friends that aren't me... I hate the thought of it. Once, I was so used to be alone that I didn't care about those kinds of things. But I think I maybe did without realising. Because now that I have someone in my corner, I don't want to let them go.

But that's what happens in life. People come and then they go. Sometimes, they don't ever come back.

"Hey, Mum," I whisper. I put the flowers into the fresh water and slot it back in to the headstone; it looks much brighter now, much more accurate of how she would want it to be. "I got you some flowers; they don't look as good as yours, though."

Silence.

"I'm starting sixth form soon, the same one you went to," I tell her, sitting cross-legged on the grass like I'm a little kid again. "I won't have any friends there yet but I'm going to try and make some. I don't want to be alone anymore. I hope you're not... I know you felt like you were at one point. You did one of the hardest things all by yourself but I'm really glad you did. I couldn't have asked for a better Mum. Oh, I found a record that you would have loved! It's got some of Cher's old songs on it; the ones you used to sing all the time. You had such a beautiful voice; I hope I can still picture it by the time I can afford a record player."

I laugh a little at this like she would have done.

"I'll always think of you when I hear her music," I continue. "Or whenever I see flowers. I'll make sure that you always have some; then people will know how loved you were – *are*. I want people to remember you like you're alive still; like they could go into your florist shop and pick a bouquet out. And I'll always try and find ways to remember you. Because..."

I sniffle, wishing she could hear me say this.

"Because I will never forget you, Mum."

Acknowledgements

After I published *Lost for You*, I was completely ready to dive into a new story, except this took a turn I wasn't quiet expecting. What started out as an exploration of a teenager struggling with anxiety became something else entirely; a daughter struggling to cope with the aftermath of losing her Mum.

This was a very difficult topic to write about, especially when someone very inspirational to me passed away only a few weeks into the process. But with the sadness came an overwhelming amount of love from all the people who she had touched. And so I am very honoured to be able to dedicate the book to her because, as it says, she will never be forgotten.

In terms of who I would like to thank, I have found support in so many people for this particular book.

Thank you to Emma Smith for the most perfect book cover and for the insane amount of hours you spent designing the graphics. They really do make a world of difference and I love seeing your ideas. I also really appreciate all the kindness you have given and for being such a wonderful and inspiring writer and friend.

Thank you to George Somers for the poem at the start of this book. You have always been the most amazing best friend and I am so proud of you, just as I know she will be.

Thank you to Em Solstice for all the advice and motivation throughout the writing stage. It's so amazing to be able to talk to someone who understands how hard it is to self-publish.

I would also like to thank the online community for all the love for *Lost for You* over these last few months and for the genuine care some of you have shown. It's really exciting and I am so grateful!

Thank you as well to my family, friends and boyfriend. As usual, you have listened to my long rambles about my books, writing and ideas because I'm such a chatterbox.

~ Faith

faith fawcett

Faith has always been an avid reader with a love for writing. Her favourite memories are those moments when she was tucked up in bed with characters like Anne of Green Gables and Hetty Feather!

books for children:

- The Witch's Kitten
- The Broomstick Trials
- The Winter Wizard

books for young adults:

- Felicity
- Adelaide
- Lost For You

Faith Fawcett Author on Facebook
@faith3699 on TikTok
@_faith_fawcett_author on Instagram

Printed in Great Britain
by Amazon